Wrath of the Demiurge

Wind of Destiny, Volume Five

AJ Cooper

Wrath of the Demiurge
Copyright © 2017 Andrew James Cooper
Published by Realms of Varda
www.vardabooks.com

All Rights Reserved. No part of this book may be reproduced, scanned, or distributed in any print or electronic form without permission.

All characters appearing in this work are fictitious. Any resemblance to real persons, living or dead, is purely coincidental.

Front cover art © Breakermaximus | Dreamstime.com

Back cover art © Desislava Vasileva | Dreamstime.com

ISBN 978-1-958724-04-0

Eloesus
100 mi. 200 mi. 300 mi. 400 mi. 500 mi.
SANCTON
THE BLESSED ISLES
RIVER SULIS
PALLISTRIX
ISTEROS
ARCTOS
AGATHE
TIGRIS
IOGHEIRA
STRAITEIRA
THÉNAI
THENOA
KERSEPOLI
KERSICA
KORTHOS
KORTHICA
TEN CITIES
THARTA
THARTICA
ARKADIOS
THEMURIA

THE VOICE OF THE DEMIURGE

The veil was opened.

Gaia had opened it.

Beyond the shimmering portal lay a world of fire: red mountains amid a boiling sulfur sea. The sky was yellow; and even from far away, the heat emanating from this portal was enough to make Gaia sweat.

The portal was weakening by the second. It was shrinking in size and every few moments, blinked out of existence altogether.

The government of Korthos, gathered before Gaia's masterwork, was transfixed by the sight. The machine which had opened this doorway between worlds—the dreaded Gammahedron—had begun to smoke.

And then out of nowhere, a ghostly hand materialized, reaching out from the portal. In substance it was like smoke; it pointed to the crowd, and then to Gaia.

"You have awoken me!" shouted a voice. "You have given me a foothold!"

The Gammahedron screeched as its inner workings began to fail. The portal blinked out of existence and the engine caught fire. The Gammahedron was burning.

But the faces that met Gaia were full of awe.

She had regained their respect. She was back in command. She would conquer the city again, with or without Rogon's help.

TRUTH

"What is truth?" asked the philosopher underneath the olive tree.

The student didn't know what to say. He had read the books which his teacher had asked. He had studied every night in the hopes of achieving his diploma—in the words of his father, "a mere parchment scroll." He had spent every last *doukos* on the Academy; he'd be damned if he failed now. "I don't know," he admitted.

"Admitting your ignorance is the first step," said the philosopher.

"There is no answer. There is no truth."

OUTSIDE KORTHOS

To say Rogon and Gaia's relationship had soured was an understatement verging on blasphemy.

Rogon did not particularly mind. This gimmick with the "Gammahedron" might impress the Assembly briefly, but she had no true leverage over them.

In his homeland, there was a saying: "better three armies encamped against me, than my queen full of wrath."

But Gaia did not know Rogon. The Assembly and the archon did not know Rogon.

If any of them truly knew him, they'd never fight by his side.

~

The House of Assembly in Korthos had become Rogon's home, but his compatriots there knew better than anyone else how uncomfortable it made him.

He was a man of the battlefield. He was not suited to politicking, to whispers, to backstabbing, to plots and coups. He spoke his mind—a thing which stunned even the Korthian commoners.

It was here, in the House of Assembly, that a council of war had been convened.

Here Rogon stood. There were seven Strategoi around a circular table, seven commanders of the Kersican League army. The mood in the chamber was already dour.

Rogon knew the words before they came out of Septimon's mouth.

"The battle at Dimos is lost," he said. "Ten thousand Kersican hoplites scattered like cowards... before the Thenoan

Army. The 'Free and Democratic Army of Thénai!'"

The mood was one of incredulity. Rogon knew what these Eloesians thought of the Kersican army… it was supposedly undefeatable.

The Eloesians thought these heavily trained hoplites could never fail… these men who were taken at a young age from their mothers, brainwashed and turned into killing machines.

But Rogon knew the advantages Thénai had… the morale which this "Free and Democratic Army" possessed could overcome the best-equipped, best-trained warriors in the land. He had learned not to underestimate the power of an army convinced of its own righteousness… convinced that the gods favored them above others. To destroy the morale would take overwhelming force, force which—it seemed—the Kersican League lacked entirely.

If they had failed to take the small, but strategic town of Dimos, this war between the Kersican and the Thenoan Leagues would grind to a deadly stalemate… and before it ended, everyone would be counted a loser.

"Something must be done," said Rogon, "something drastic."

What had been stewing in his thoughts for months had bubbled to the surface. An alliance with the southrons against the Thenoan League would push them to the breaking point. With the King of Kings' help, Thénai would fall, and the Free and Democratic Army… the "small but righteous band" would be crushed under the foot of a vastly stronger foe.

But now was not the time. The hatred for the southrons burned deep.

It would take more humiliations to wear down their resistance to the idea, more degradations and massacres.

Eventually they would have no choice but to listen to

reason.

The sword of the Kersican would be replaced with the scimitar of the southron. When they reached the breaking point, no bent knee, no prostrate bow, no worship of the padisha, would be spared to seek victory.

HOUSE OF ASSEMBLY, THÉNAI

Amid a slew of bad news, Hyron—de facto leader of the Thenoan League—had taken comfort at the unexpected victory in Dimos.

For ages the walled city of Dimos had stood guard and never failed, watching over the merchants and citizens who passed along the road.

The Kersican Army had new tactics and even greater siege weapons than before. Yet somehow, the garrison of five-thousand Free and Democratic soldiers had withstood the thirty-day assault, and at last driven them from the city altogether.

The news would no doubt be met with horror in Korthos.

Against the wishes of King Kunar he had reconvened an Assembly. A special election had been held; the two hundred of the best and brightest in Thénai had been chosen.

Delegates from all the tributary cities combined to make up a body of four hundred officials.

Hyron, as deputy for King Kunar, had theoretically unlimited power. But as a Thenoan, he believed above all in democracy. Nothing could be decided without the will of the people.

Hyron passed through the double doors of the House floor.

Above him on the ceiling, a great mosaic had been inscribed in dazzling color. At a cost of twenty *talents*, the unlikely victories of the Southron War had been displayed. With millions of glass pieces, a stunning portrayal of the Battle of Maratha was depicted: a hundred horsemen in Thenoan armor charging the fleeing southrons—the mighty hero Theron astride a chariot with the sword and helm of Phillipidēs in his hands.

But Theron was gone, now. He would never come back. He had disappeared into the ether… he was a footnote in history, a powerful symbol of the city's return to glory, and a symbol only.

In the mosaic, Rogon—the one called the Dark Captain—was portrayed wounded and running away.

But out of the ashes, the Dark Captain had arisen. He had butchered the people of Nissos. Callous and cruel was Rogon; the list of those slain by him were without number. If Hyron did not stop him, he would put all of Eloesus to the sword.

He felt a cool breeze behind him. The doors had opened again, and standing there was a man dressed in rugged browns and grays, with a blue sash over his shoulder.

"Speaker," said the man. "A message from the border."

Hyron did not want to hear any more bad news.

This messenger might do his heart in.

"Speak," he said.

"An army is gathering just outside the river," he said. "Ten thousand now, but growing by the day. Prince Sébastion is worried."

Bastos Tower guarded the way into Thenoa from the Brown River. It had held firm against Thénai's enemies for hundreds of years. No one could deny the development was worrying.

But Hyron did not act without the advice of his compatriots.

At the top of the Assembly House, above the roof, was a bell which they had refurbished and gilded at a cost of four-hundred *doukon*. Its sound and timbre were unique and carried all across the city of Thénai. Hyron rang it three times to summon the Assembly, and a fourth to indicate its urgency.

His two hundred fellow demiarchs, plus his two-hundred representatives from across the Thenoan League, would be here soon.

~

The Assembly's session began with a furor when Hyron explained the situation.

One, a delegate from the isle of Pos, began shouting nonsense about how his people wished for no more bloodshed. "Each year, we give you a *talent* from our treasury! That is more money than you deserve!"

"We must enlarge our army," said Hyron.

His spies had told him the Kersicans outspend them, two to one. The Thenoans had greater wealth, but the Kersicans had a greater army, which grew by the day.

His words caused the fury to blow up beyond what he had feared. The shouting grew so loud, their concerns had become inaudible.

"Enough!" Hyron had a way of silencing these loudly bickering children. In an instant, they had quieted completely; Hyron could hear his own breath. "I have tried over and over to convince you."

"There is not enough gold in the treasury," said one of the few demiarchs Hyron trusted, Geon.

And Geon's words were true.

The loss of Nissos had been devastating, and now even the loyalty of the tributary cities they already had were tapering. Much of the wealth had already been spent on beautifying the city… and the High City was being raised another two-hundred feet so that it would be the highest in Eloesus.

The Thenoans, ever dreamers and artists, knew how to spend their money.

The truth of the statement weighed heavy on Hyron.

"We need new allies," said Hyron. "We need more allies."

"We need Tharta," said Geon.

There was truth in Geon's words.

Once the superpower of Eloesus, they had retreated into the shadows after they failed to act in the Southron War. But they still had great wealth and a people as numerous as the stars in the sky. In an instant, Hyron had become convinced of the course he must take.

"I will go to Tharta," said Hyron. "We will convince King Gygax to join the Thenoan League."

HOUSE OF THE SATYR, KORTHOS

Still exulting in her accomplishment and her meteoric rise from disgrace, Gaia looked forward to the best night of sleep she'd ever had.

She spread out the sheets of Khazidean linen. She laid out sprigs of aromatic hyrkanthus leaves and perfumed it with aloes and myrrh. She set out a pillow lined with clean white cotton, and—unclipping the brace on her gown—entered the elysium of her bed unclothed.

She drank deep of a glass of red wine. She uttered a prayer of thanksgiving to fortune and to whatever forces of reality conspired to renew her and put her back on top.

Then, filled with hope and optimism, she shut her eyes and slipped away into sleep and into another world, into a deep and intoxicating dream.

~

In the heart of this dream, she was in her bed awake. The air had turned cold and she could not move. Paralyzed, she could not resist or struggle, she could not flee. Out of the shadows of her closet arose a dark shape, a black silhouette shaped like a man of war. His being radiated cold, and in the midst of the black darkness of his face two red fires, like eyes, burned into existence.

The walls of Gaia's bedroom seemed to pulse, and the sound of her breath was like the quaking of the earth.

She struggled and tried to scream, but could not move as the shadow man approached and then loomed over her.

The shadow man touched her hand. His touch was like ice.

"Who art thou?"

In a panic, Gaia remembered the voice… the voice she had heard after opening the portal to another world. This was the creature whose hand had pointed to her, who now knew her, whose hand now touched hers.

She wanted to scream but she was immobile and helpless before this creature of shadow.

"What is thy name?"

With its left hand the creature touched Gaia's head, sending waves of ice and cold through her veins. She shrieked but no sound came out.

"Gaia," said the shadow man.

She fought and struggled harder than she ever had. She spit and cursed and tried to move. It was all for naught.

"I will see thee soon," said the shadow man.

Released from the spell, Gaia sat up on her bed, covered in sweat.

Her cat Ira scurried away.

Had Ira been possessed by this spirit? Had this shadow man been indwelling precious Ira?

Gaia dared not go back to sleep tonight.

She was trembling. Perhaps she would purchase some charm or amulet. But what could protect her from a being so powerful, a being which she herself had called into the world?

GATE OF STORMS, KORTHOS

Rogon did not spend any more time in the city than he needed to.

He could not bear the cynical, backstabbing politicians of Korthos, the way they said one thing to the public and then did something else entirely behind their backs.

Yes, there was intrigue back home, in southron lands, but he had been far from it. The King of Kings with his hundreds of courtiers, hundreds of wives and his hundreds of children, had to be cautious at all times.

Out of the Gate of Storms he went, and into the countryside.

Where once, Korthian citizens labored in vineyards and tilled the wheat fields, now soldiers practiced drills. By Rogon's advice, the Korthians had doubled their army, and then doubled it again.

While the limp-bodied pederasts of Thénai spent every last *talent* on sculpture and art and decoration, Rogon had forced the Kersican League to be practical. An effeminate statue carved by a great sculptor would cost the same as a hundred helmets or a dozen well-forged swords. A bronze likeness of a hoplite could pay the salary of ten real ones.

Though the warriors of Eloesus fought bravely, Rogon had gained precious little respect for this land. It focused far too much on things that mattered little, and too little on things that mattered much. In Fharas, there were no plays or actors. The King of Kings listened not at all to music, nor was he entertained by storytellers.

And yet, somehow, on the Fields of Maratha, Rogon had failed.

He had failed against the disgraced commander Theron. Theron, whom he had come to detest.

It was a matter of honor, now, to crush the Thenoan League. It was a matter of revenge, of regaining his manhood. He would see Theron's forces brought to ruin.

But things, as they stood, were at a stalemate. He had ordered the formation of an army at the border. This decoy army was a distraction; another army was being formed of Kersepolan hoplites, together with the hundred Chosen, and King Helion.

With the largest army they could muster, they would wind around the mountain road and attack the Thenoan heartland in a sudden surprise. Through Arkadion they would march, even in the snow.

All these men sprinting across obstacles and shooting arrows at targets were his. He had appointed Strategoi and outfitted them with the best of arms and armor.

Yet their victory was not certain. If he could convince King Helion and his compatriot to join forces with the southrons, the Thenoan League wouldn't stand a chance.

A desire was burning in him, brighter and hotter than any flame in this world. He had to reclaim his revenge.

Theron had slipped away and vanished from sight, but he would find the so-called "hero of the Southron War" and tear him to bits. He would see Theron drawn and quartered, his body left to lie and picked apart by flesh flies.

And Thénai would burn.

~

In the night, far from the noise of the camps, Rogon cleared the brush in a wide circle until the dirt was bare. With stones he built an altar, laying one on top of the other. On top of the altar he laid dried sticks he had gathered, dried-out pine boughs and wilted leaves, grasses and the brush he had removed with his knife. On top of the brush he laid the heart of a lamb. With a flint and tinder, he lit a torch.

The god of fire, Athra, was worshipped by the King of Kings and all in his court.

But Rogon's god was more ancient than Athra. The history of his god went back to forgotten times, when man did not live in houses or farm crops. The history of his nameless god went back to the time when man wandered the wilderness like packs of wolves, roaming from one place to another.

The nameless god which Rogon worshipped demanded blood. His god was the true god of fire. With a head like a serpent's and the body of an ascended immortal he ruled over those lesser than he. The priests had suppressed his worship; but he was not forgotten—even if his name had been scrubbed from memory.

"To the nameless god I swear," Rogon said, and tossed the torch onto the altar. Flame exploded into existence on the altar, licking away every last bit of moisture. Rogon could almost hear the voices of the night calling out to him. "To the nameless god I make an oath… to vanquish this Theron, to see him dead and dishonored. And if not, then drag me to the depths of hell."

He thrust his left hand into the fire until he could bear the heat no longer.

The burn would plague him for weeks. He had endured far worse. The oath was set; he could not abandon his promise. His master was a vengeful one. There would be no mercy for him if he failed.

ROYAL THARTA GATE, THARTA

Two Weeks Later…

This massive gate, stretching high above Hyron, was white as alabaster, carved in scenes of a war between the new and old gods. It was called a wonder of the world throughout Eloesus; it had been etched from the whitest of marble in ancient days. No city gate could compare to the Royal Tharta Gate, not even Lion's Gate back home. Tharta's wealth was as ancient as Thénai's was new. It had been the greatest city in Eloesus; now, its borders were silent.

With Tharta's help, the Thenoan League might prevail. The war might end altogether, with Tharta's backing.

Flanked by hoplites and his entourage, Hyron pushed ahead, through the open gate and into the heart of Eloesus' most ancient city.

The city was different.

Very different.

The streets seemed worn, the pavestones on the roads washed away in places. The people of Tharta looked at Hyron with a mix of confusion and disgust, as if they expected no foreigners at all.

And there were Fharese people here: women, with their heads covered, in gowns of bright blue silk, men with bushy black beards. They mixed in with the crowds of Eloesians without incident.

As Hyron passed down the way, there was a bronze statue set up; its arms were outstretched and the statue itself seemed blazing hot, on verge of being molten.

Fharese men and women were gathered there, and Ten Cities men in pointed caps. They were crying out: *"Ya Melkior! Ya Melkior!"*

Eloesians, too, were standing before the statue, crying out the foreign adulation, wearing pointed Megarine caps. A gong was rung, and the *"Ya Melkior! Ya Melkior!"* turned to a frenzy.

To Hyron's horror something was flung onto the scalding-hot hands of the idol. It couldn't be an infant… it couldn't be. It had to be a lamb.

He looked away and pressed on through the streets. Pipesmoke was emanating from many of the houses.

Under King Gygax, things had changed. Things had changed greatly.

No longer was Tharta a great city of Eloesian culture, but now a black spot on the earth, a southron slum.

When he entered the Royal Square in view of the palace, the Fharese outnumbered the Eloesians two to one. Fharese maidens with their heads uncovered laughed with Fharese youths. Married women who covered their hair were purchasing goods from the hundreds of vendors. The air was thick with the scent of cinnamon and cardamom.

Hyron continued on his path through the once-great city of Tharta. King Gygax had consented to meet; he had no illusions that forming an alliance would be easy, but he had hope. With Tharta's power, the Kersican League would falter; the war would end, and a stalemate would preclude peace.

An Eloesian was shouting near the palace gate. He was wearing traditional dress—a white chiton and sandals—and waving a sword. "Go home, southrons! You do not belong here! Go home! I am a Thartan, you are not!"

The Fharese did not seem bothered by the disruption; they

were ignoring him completely. Women and men both paid him no heed.

This, Hyron thought, was the common man's last stand before the long-hailed "Fharaization" of Tharta.

At the gates to the palace, hoplites in full regalia recognized the entourage and stepped aside. Into the palace Hyron went, into the home of Gygax King of Tharta.

~

Through a gateway wrought of gold, through a hall of colored tile—lined with paintings of ancient artists—they came to a courtyard perfumed with the scent of garden plants. Benches wrought of silver lined the courtyard. Two women sat on one, their heads covered; one was clearly pregnant, and the other watched her child play with some gizmo. Across the courtyard a woman who wore her hair free was chasing toddling children around.

It had become clear: the palace of Gygax was filled with children.

The hoplites led them through the perfumed courtyard, beyond a gateway of pointed arches. More women and more children were in the rooms ahead; it dawned on him, in all the scandal, that these women were Gygax's wives.

He had spurned Eloesians' most sacred tradition—that one man should be with one wife.

In southron lands, Hyron had heard of men with four or five wives, usually the richest of them all; but judging by the palace, Gygax's wives could reach a hundred. The children were without count.

What had happened to Gygax's first wife, Zubeida?

Hyron was led further into the heart of the palace and he saw the wives were not only southron but of all peoples. There were blonde women and brown haired women, white and tan and ebony. King Gygax had picked his wives from all over the world.

Together with women and children were slaves doting on their every need, marked by iron collars and brown, undyed woolen clothing. The population of the palace could easily be in the thousands.

Past golden busts and silver chalices, past priceless masterworks hanging on the marble walls, the throne room opened up before Hyron.

King Gygax sat on the titanic silver and emerald throne, and though he was an ant before it, his figure was clearly distinguishable by the golden sunray crown he wore. He did not rise when he saw Hyron and his entourage. He sat there, wearing a purple robe, his fingers covered in jeweled rings. By his side, on a smaller throne forged of silver and rubies, was a woman Hyron recognized as Zubeida. She remained the wife whom Gygax favored above all others.

When Hyron reached the foot of the throne, he hesitated. Protocol told him to fall prostrate in obeisance or bow to the ground.

But he was the leader of Thénai in all but name; while King Kunar drank himself into a stupor, he represented the city and its interests.

He did not bow or fall to his face. He stood up and met Gygax's gaze, head-on.

Gygax was not the boyish king he remembered. There were bags under his eyes and too many wrinkles for his age.

Hyron could not imagine the stress of having a hundred wives. Grapheia gave him enough trouble as it was.

Gygax was glaring at Hyron. *How dare this Thenoan not fall prostrate?* Hyron had a feeling negotiations would be tough. But he would not debase his city, he would not dishonor it. He would not show any sign of deference, even to the King of Tharta.

Hoplites flanked either side of the throne. These hoplites were different from the others. The horsehair crests on their helms were dark purple; their armor was polished and glinted in the light of the skylight above. In one hand they held glaives like those of the amazons; in the other bulky tower shields which touched the ground. This was the Royal Guard.

"Bow," they said in unison.

But Hyron stood firm. "Thénai won the Southron War. As its leader, I dare to say we are equals."

Fury engulfed the throne room. Hoplites in standard gear drew their swords. They were ready to spill blood but Gygax raised his hand and ordered them to stop.

"We will hear the fool out," said Gygax. "And if we do not like what we hear, then we will cut off his tongue."

What to say? How to put it? This was the most important moment of Hyron's life. So much rested on this, on this moment. "I come to make you an offer," he said. "An alliance, to make Tharta great and feared once again…"

THRONE ROOM, THARTAN PALACE

Gygax sat there in his royal splendor, saying nothing after Hyron's offer.

His wife was regarding Hyron and his entourage coldly. The southron beauty clearly had her husband's ear.

"Thénai has made clear its hatred for Fharas," Gygax said, "whereas Tharta and the Ten Cities have pledged to become part of the Southron World.

"Your democracy is an offense to government. People who live in utter ignorance are allowed to have their say, to cast their vote and pick whoever promises them the most. To join hands with the Thenoan League would sully our name forever. You chose to go to war against the Kersican League; your wars are your own. Leave Tharta out of it."

His wife stood up from her throne. "My love… a word."

Gygax shouted to his guards, "Make sure they don't go anywhere!"

~

When he returned it seemed he was a chained man, a puppy which his wife Zubeida led about on a leash. Most marriages ended up that way.

Again King Gygax took his seat on the Silver Throne. "We have heard you out. Now, go. You might hear from me. You might not. Goodbye."

THE OLD MOUNTAIN ROAD, OUTSIDE THEMURIA

They had marched a week in grueling conditions, but Rogon loved the struggle and the exertion. Exhausted, he continued on, leading his battalion at the front. All his treasured belongings he had laid on his horse; he had donned his armor and in his armor he had marched. The cold winds were blowing from the mountains. Yesterday, a snow flurry had caught them unawares. It had ended quickly, but what a wonder—Rogon had never seen anything like it before.

Before he left the lowland, he had dispatched spies all across Eloesus, including those who professed allegiance to the Thenoan League. As soon as they discovered the whereabouts of Theron, they would tell Rogon; and Rogon would hunt him down and hoist his head on a pike.

And unrest had overcome the ranks. There was building tension between the Korthians, who called the Kersicans brutes and thugs, and the Kersicans who bragged ceaselessly about their military prowess. The army was fraying at the seams. Only their undying respect for Rogon bound them together. They had absolute confidence in him; they believed they would receive an equal share of the spoils. They believed Rogon cared about the Kersican League, even that he had gained a love for the Eloesian people. They believed so much.

That night a storm swept in, and to the soldiers' dread, snow began to fall, and fall, and fall. Rogon, in his heavy winter coat, was shivering and in misery as one of the Strategoi tried, and failed, to start a fire.

Such misery these lowlanders had never experienced before. Rogon feared they had not adequately prepared for the struggles ahead. Perhaps the experts they relied on did not realize the full gravity of the situation. Taking the Old Mountain Road in winter would surprise the Thenoans, because the Thenoans would have thought it impossible.

What if it was?

After an hour of cursing and furiously working the flint and tinder, the brush burst into flame and the logs caught on. The slow-burning wood melted away the snow, and life-giving warmth helped take the edge off the winter's night.

No soldier wanted to speak. No stories were told. They rubbed their hands near the fire.

Rogan sensed they feared doom. A harsh path lay ahead. But Rogon would lead them to safety, and then to victory. He had no doubts. He had never failed at anything before. Everything his god had set before him, he had accomplished. He had never tasted defeat.

~

A blizzard slowed their progress to a standstill the next day. Rogon had never braved such misery.

He could barely see a foot ahead of him. He had come to realize, for all this difficulty he himself was having, most Eloesians had never experienced this. These men in his army were flatlanders, not Arkadians; they were dwellers in the coastal cities who regarded the rustics with scorn.

Perhaps now they would gain some respect for these hardy people who lived through the winter, who braved the blizzards and freezing winds. To endure this for even an hour took an enormous constitution.

As the day wore on, and the snow reached Rogon's knee, he began to wonder if the impossible could happen.

He began to wonder if he would fail.

THE HOUSE OF THE SATYR, KORTHOS

In the evening, Gaia had the misfortune of eating dinner with her husband.

They had made it a point not to, but sometimes their paths inexplicably crossed.

He knew very well of her affair with Rogon. He did not care about the betrayal, or about her. He cared that it had become widespread knowledge.

He would be known as Rogon's cuckold. This harmed his own political ambitions.

Not to mention his wife was loud and boisterous, full of ambition, everything an Eloesian wife shouldn't be.

"Are you going to eat your lamb?" she said.

Not only had she seasoned the lamb shanks and spent three hours cooking it slowly, she had offered him her favorite wine which she had bought herself.

Arkedamon wouldn't even look at her.

"I am sorry for what happened." Her mercy surprised her. How many times had he tossed her aside for his own benefit, especially in the early days, when they were just private citizens angling for power? She was no saint, but he had a monstrous side too.

Arkedamon finally met her gaze. "Will you let me eat in peace?"

"Eat the lamb I spent hours preparing... the wine which cost ten *doukon*?"

"We spend no time together for years... living in the same house... in different rooms... and suddenly we are loving man and wife, because Rogon spurned you?"

The insult of Rogon's rejection caused a flash of anger to well up within her, but she held her tongue. "This has nothing to do with that dumb brute…"

"Ah, so now you hate him. You can't have him, so you hate him."

What had she expected from her "husband?" Their marriage had been a pact from the beginning, a show. They had lain together, yes, but not for years. He had pursued courtesans and whores alike; she had bedded others. How could she expect a warm welcome, a kind word, even after laboring so hard in the kitchen? How could she expect anything from Arkedamon except hatred?

There was no rekindling that friendship, that alliance. It had been destroyed never to recover.

She took her plate and her goblet and went upstairs, out onto the porch overlooking the city. She was a stranger in her own home, and a stranger she would remain. She ate and drank in solitude, observing the street below.

~

At night, grief weighed heavy on her.

She lay there in the covers a long while, trying to forget about everything.

She had gained some modicum of respect from the Assembly after creating the Astral Gate. But it had profited neither her nor them hardly at all. What was a modicum of respect, when vast respect was required to regain her former power?

The Astral Gate was worthless. All that effort was for naught. So be it.

She blew out her bedside candle and some time later, fell asleep.

In the middle of the night, she awoke, unable to move. The room had grown cold, and horror dawned on Gaia as she remembered what had happened to her before—what was happening now.

Unable to move, she lay there, wanting to close her eyes but failing. She was controlled by some dark force. It seemed she had become heavy and sunk into the bed.

She was colder than she had ever been in the throes of the worst winter. When she breathed, fog emerged from her mouth.

And then he appeared, just as she thought he would.

The silhouette of darkness was the shape of a man in armor. From his pitch-black face there beamed two burning red eyes. He drew closer and as much as Gaia wanted to flee, he continued walking until he had reached the edge of her bed, and was looming over her.

"Thou art the one I touched… the one which I saw beyond the veil. Thou art the one blessed by me… blessed by the touch of the demiurge."

He waved a hand of pure shadow above her. She wanted to scream but lay as motionless as a corpse.

"Tell me what thou seekest… and I shall give it to thee."

When the shadow man touched her, her heart exploded into fury. She wanted to weep and wail. She could do nothing. Even without his prompting, she could sense this creature was reading her thoughts, was drawing inspiration from all the hidden compartments of her mind.

"Power is what thou seekest above all. And power I shall give to thee. Thou must stoop down and worship me…"

She could not speak. She could not respond. She would not worship him.

This was not a nightmare. This was a curse which she could not escape by her own will. This being she had contacted from beyond the Astral Portal… it had gained a foothold in her mind.

She tried to scream and tried to struggle, but she could not do anything except lie still.

Who was this creature? Who was this entity? Who was the demiurge, and what did it want from her?

~

When the nightmare ended and when she returned to normal sleep, she could not remember the next morning. At some point the phantom had left her, the phantom which called itself the demiurge.

Her heart beat fast though the daylight was filtering in through the windows and the urban noise had begun. The rattling of carts, the shouts of passersby, the barks of dogs and the noise of streetside vendors could not erase the memory of the vivid dream. This was no ordinary dream she had experienced, but a possession by dark forces.

Demiurge. Where had she heard that word before? It was faintly familiar. Who had said it? Where had she read it?

She donned her undergarments and then a gown of gold cloth. She wrapped her waist with a glinting silver sash.

Looking in the mirror, she touched up her face with cosmetics. She had become pale, almost to the point of deathliness. She brushed her cheeks with rose powder and dabbed her eyelashes with black ink-of-Tyrhenos. She ran a comb through her hair.

She felt in danger in this room, even by herself, even in broad daylight.

She had become cursed. She had never believed in such things before. But she had to free herself of it. She had to purge this delusion from her mind. It could not be real; there had to be some explanation.

Down the busy street and around the corner was the neighborhood apothecary. She could not count the number of times she had purchased medicines, potions and elixirs for various ailments. Harkon knew exactly what she needed, with the vaguest of descriptions. Just last year, he had cured a stomachache and then a headache with his potions. In Gaia's three decades of life, he had prescribed two abortifacients—something she was not proud of. It remained a fact that Harkon was a miracle worker, a magician in all but name.

In Harkon's shop—behind a desk—there were shelves and shelves of jars and pots, labeled in eccentric style—Some said "For stomachaches" others "for fever" or "for pox" while others had scribbled on them "Mixture number thirteen" or "Brewed queen-of-the-evening and lemon balm." All the erratic mixtures he had brewed or powdered together were labeled with notes only he could understand.

She could smell smoke and some horridly foul mixture being brewed beyond the shelves. She rang a bell on the desk and quickly Harkon appeared, dressed in a tunic stained with smoke and grime. He was always hard at work.

"Gaia!" said Harkon. "Hello, beautiful."

He looked surprised. He had reason to be surprised. Ordinarily, Gaia sent her servants to fetch whatever was required. But now was different. This problem she had was not something she would readily admit. It verged on embarrassing. "A word in private?" she said.

Harkon smiled. Perhaps he thought Gaia suffered from some woman's trouble which she dared not describe in public. If only that were true.

Harkon took her behind the desk and into his workroom,

which was filled with vials and cauldrons. In a small cauldron underneath a fire, the foul mixture she smelled was bubbling. In the hot water there were sprigs of some plant mixed together with the tentacles of a squid. She pitied whoever was unlucky enough to require the potion.

"What troubles you, my Gaia?" asked Harkon.

"A dream."

At her description, Harkon gasped. "I'm not sure if it is anything a potion can cure… maybe you should go to the temple."

The temple! Gaia wanted to laugh. She had never cared much for the priests, stealing money from the vulnerable, collecting silver and gold in their offering trays. She was not sure if the gods in heaven were true, but she was certain—if they did exist—that they had no pity or care for mankind. Everything could be explained through logic.

But she did have cause to wonder after the horror of last night. Her mind told her it was a delusion, easily cured by one of Harkon's brews. Her heart told her the phantom was something she should dread, something she should fear and run from. "You must have something," she said.

"Go to a temple… ask to be cleansed."

The suggestion enraged her. She had worked so hard to pass a law banning street preachers and religious madmen. Now she was being preached to. "Do you really believe—"

"I don't know," Harkon said.

She had thought better of him. If he would not help her, perhaps somebody would. "There is one other thing Harkon…"

He glanced at her curiously.

"He called himself the demiurge."

Harkon took a step back. "Get out!" he shouted. "Get out of here, and never come back…"

CITY SQUARE, THÉNAI

The journey back to the city Hyron loved seemed quicker than the journey to Tharta.

The most ancient of Eloesian cities had changed irrevocably, and the king did not have a queen but instead a southron harem.

The sky was cloudy and rain was pouring down. The air's wintry chill had propelled Hyron to don his coat for the first time this year. The people in the square were as downcast as the sky.

Something had changed. Something horrible.

Instinctively he looked up to the High City and the Temple of Tyros, and to the House of the Archon where the king dwelled.

Surrounded by hoplites and a bevy of government officials, he could see by their concerned faces that they sensed it too. Something was amiss in Thénai.

After speaking with his fellow demiarchs, he learned what troubled the king, and by extension the people.

A rumor had spread across the countryside that Theron, the disgraced veteran of the Southron War, was returning, and with an army.

King Kunar had responded with corresponding violence, throwing those demiarchs who formerly supported Theron in prison.

Did he know Hyron also had argued for him and supported him all this time?

And he still could not believe the news. He was certain of Theron's death, and nothing could convince him otherwise. His spies were mistaken.

He had to speak to the king himself.

The arduous upward path to the city's highest point was taxing for Hyron's old bones. However, he made the journey like he always had. His wife Grapheia would be proud; but she rarely saw him. Grapheia was one of the last traditional wives of Thénai; never leaving home, going outside only rarely, even going so far as to cover her hair. Her kind were quickly passing away.

The temple to Amara, virgin queen, had been replaced with an abomination—the new Temple of Tyros, dedicated on Third Night of 316. The statue of Amara had been decapitated, her head replaced with that of a bear; the jewels which once adorned her gold cloak fashioned into gleaming, predatory eyes.

And beside the temple lay the House of the Archon, which grew in size and grandeur seemingly with each passing day. Servants had labored for weeks building a colonnade of white marble and growing between the columns were brightly colored rose bushes. Surrounding the colonnade and the House of the Archon, a plaza of brightly colored tiles gleamed in the sun, glinting their patterns of red, green and white. Such splendor had long been considered too showy for an archon, a democratically elected "public servant." But now Thénai had a king.

Inside the spacious halls, servants scurried this way and that. In the kitchen the clattering of pots and pans echoed at a frenetic pace. Other servants were wiping wine-stains from a rug, no doubt from one of King Kunar's drunken parties.

All throughout the House of the Archon, there were paintings of King Kunar in various poses, portraying him in full armor, with a hoplite's sword and shield—possessing bravery which, in real life, he did not have.

As King Kunar's only trusted link to the Thenoan Assembly, Hyron was privileged with the inner workings of his mind. King Kunar had seemed a stupid oaf at first—yet when he had abstained from drink, a new personality emerged. Kunar was intelligent, if hasty in decision making. He was also deeply insecure.

And yet despite him, Hyron had begun to develop some respect.

Kunar was in the hall of feasting, listening to a lutist strumming a soothing melody. He had a glass of wine in his hand, but judging by his lack of shouting and cursing, he was nowhere near drunk.

As soon as Kunar became aware of Hyron's presence, he lifted up his hand and the lutist left. All the servants and hangers-on quickly followed.

Kunar had developed an implicit trust for Hyron. "What is it?" he said, knowing already that it was important.

"You said Theron has returned…"

Some of the color drained from Kunar's face.

"Where did you learn this information? Where did your spies find it?" If Theron had risen in arms openly, Hyron would know about it.

"A maid of the Mount of Prophecy…"

In Isteros, they had as much reverence for the Oracle as any other part of Eloesus. But many even among her most devout followers believed she was fallible. How many things had she predicted which did not bear fruit? How many of her prophecies were double sided, having many interpretations and making little concrete sense? King Kunar was a man who lived in the moment, who didn't give much credence to signs, who did not despair when a crow landed near his window. So why would the word of a maid of Prophecy affect him?

"She came to me yesterday…" When Kunar gave his

description, it seemed he had been caught in a spell. His eyes gazed far beyond the room as he recalled the moment. "She was beautiful, but I knew she was a maid of the Mount of Prophecy… I could not touch her without the gods' hatred. She told me he was on a mountain outside Thénai… Mount Tharnos. She said he is raising an army. She said he wants to overthrow me…"

How to convince him this was folly?

In truth the rule of Thénai and all its possessions belonged to Theron. Kunar was a mere interloper; his role was illegitimate. Hyron still nursed hatred for him; he had killed those demiarchs, and he could not bring himself to forgive Kunar, not now, not ever. But he had a city to control, a war to win. Any instability could upset the fragile balance of things.

"Mount Tharnos," repeated Hyron. "I'll send a battalion…"

"I want you to go with them," Kunar said. "There is no one else in Thénai who I trust."

Hyron had no choice but to accept. If they did capture Theron, perhaps he could convince Kunar to spare his life.

SOMEWHERE IN THEMURIA

With snow up to his knee, Rogon continued the miserable journey. The skies overhead were dark, almost black despite the hour being noon. The guides said they were leading the army down the quickest, most efficient path, but—despite winter cloaks and thick boots—more than a thousand men had perished since the journey began. Nine thousand remained, but many were on the threshold of death. Frostbite had taken some, and though the physicians knew how to help, many of them were taking ill.

Openly, people talked about the folly of their situation; but Rogon remained convinced he had made the right decision. When they reached the lowlands, the Thenoans would be caught completely off guard. They would not have time to repair; the city would fall.

This country, however, presented dangers beyond frostbite and avalanche; there were creatures in this land which defied human description. In addition to the misery of his men, he looked out for the telltale signs—a thunderous voice, a clap of thunder, all hailing the presence of a titan. This land was enchanted; it was cursed.

They had been marching through this snow for two weeks. Each day, it seemed, they resorted to butchering a horse for meat. Hunger was something Rogon had become accustomed to. If he did not suffer equally as his men, he would not have their respect. The taste of horse was tough and foul, but he ate it alongside his men.

Nine thousand remained, but more would probably die. Rogon's toes had become numb; could it be the beginning of frostbite? He did not know.

Late in the day, as the darkness had begun to grow deeper, the lights of Arkadion appeared on a hill, in view of the peak where the mad "Oracle" lived. The snow and misery had caused their marching speed to be cut in half. What would have taken days had taken a fortnight. They were in the exact center of Themuria, halfway to their destination. For a while, they could rest.

~

The villagers of Arkadion did not resist as the army descended on their village.

Kersican soldiers laughed at the wooden temples, at the "sons of shepherds" who lived in this tiny settlement on the edge of the known world. Beyond and around it were mountains. To Kersicans and Korthians, Arkadians were the laughing stock of the world; and now, brazenly, they entered the homes of citizens and scoured them for food.

Rogon observed this from Arkadion's village square. He did not approve. Theft was inadvisable.

Yes, the Arkadians had thrown in their lot with the Thenoan League. But robbing them wouldn't help things.

Rogon turned to face what they called the Mount of Prophecy. His breath turned to fog in the wintry air.

As his soldiers set up their tents or took up lodging in the villagers' homes, an insane thought passed through his head—as insane as the woman who uttered inanities on the mountain. Would he seek her advice, in the dark of night? Surely it could not hurt; maybe it could help.

Campfires glowed like beacons in the winter night. One by one they died down, becoming beds of coals.

Rogon put a third winter coat over the ones he already wore; then, quietly, mounted a horse and headed toward the mountain's bent peak.

He had found Themuria's winter unbearable beyond words, but as Rogon traveled up the mountain there was misery beyond description. The mountain road was clogged with snow—his horse was almost up to its neck, and only wooden markers showed the way. The wind was so cold it burned like fire, exposing any skin which was not covered up.

Soon the horse's head was barely above the snow. He had to turn back. There was no choice.

Ahead, there was the sound of drums.

I'm close.

He recalled the stories about the holy temple, about how spectral drums played when the Oracle was near.

His horse was exhausted and could go no further. He dismounted, finding the snow reach his neck. Some bled through his tunic. The cold burned him, but he knew what to do.

As the magi taught him, he took a handful of black rock powder from his pocket, and, from a sling across his back, a wooden wand. He could not summon up fire through magic like they could, but he knew how to create it on his own. He struck the powder against the wooden wand and watched it burst into raging life, melting the snow around him to puddles of water.

Wherever he turned, the snow receded. He cleared the path around his horse and then continued up the steep mountain path.

Panting and exhausted, he reached the snowy courtyard where the temple lay. In addition to the spectral drums, there was the sounds of lutes, lyres, and singing voices. A fire was burning amid the ruined pillars and collapsed roof.

The wooden wand had burnt to a crisp. He dropped it from his hands, and, amid the blinding snow, approached the temple.

THE RUINED TEMPLE

There were figures by the fire's glow.

He recognized the creatures which crowded near the flame—men with hairy goat's legs and horns, satyrs. Some were strumming lyres and lutes and one was playing a pipe. At the head of them all, the Oracle lay, a snake twined around her arm and neck. Despite the cold, she was nude, but she was perfectly still—not shivering, not chattering her teeth. Her eyes, white and sightless, were looking at Rogon. He could feel it in his bones.

With the Oracle's eyes focused on him, he hesitated.

He could not remember such a moment of weakness before. Even facing death on the battlefield, he had charged ahead, giving no thought to the risks. But now, the Oracle was causing him to panic; for she saw beyond his façade, she saw his inner being. She knew the dark secrets he hid, the intentions he had for Eloesus. She knew everything.

And yet he took a step forward. If she knew him, if she could see all the dark shadows which he hid, then she knew his future; she knew what instruction to give him. He ignored the terror and the shaking of his hands, and pressed forward through the snow.

When the Oracle rose and the snake which entangled her flicked its tongue, he stopped again. He swallowed his fear a second time, and pressed ahead.

"What do you seek, Rogon son of Norgon?" Her voice carried throughout the temple grounds; it seemed to permeate the air.

"I seek wisdom," said Rogon. "I seek direction. I seek truth…"

The satyrs turned to face him, revealing scraggly beards which glowed orange in the firelight. How nice it would be to draw close to the fire, to bask in the warmth amid the snow. But Rogon was too afraid of the Oracle and her power. He wanted to back away, despite the bitter wind and the blowing snow.

"You seek wisdom… wisdom I will give you." Her voice carried above the wind, piercing like a siren's call through the snow. "You seek to destroy the Thenoan League… but there is one who will destroy *you*. Theron is rising up, challenging even the Mount of Prophecy; kill him first, and I will give you the world…"

Rogon fell backward, convinced by her words. There was a flash of lightning and a crack of thunder. He turned and ran through the path he had cut through the snow, which already reached his ankle. He would kill Theron, as he wanted to; and then, he would take the world.

FISHERS STREET, KORTHOS

With buildings crowding out the sky, this narrow street in Korthos where Gaia had never been before was exceptionally dark and gloomy. Bits of pavement from prior decades covered part of it, but much had eroded to dirt. It was here, the grand librarian had told her, where she could discover the identity of the demiurge.

"I do not know," the librarian had told her, "but I sold a book to a man from Fishers Street…"

From city records, she had determined where the purchaser—a man named Barachos—had taken up residence. He was a foreigner, not a Korthian citizen. He had taken refuge in the city after the Southron War. Why he would purchase a book on ancient Eloesian history—and at a cost of some ten *doukon*—was beyond her. Yet now, this Barachos of Fishers Street possessed the only surviving copy of "The Ancient Ones of Stygia."

She continued down the dirty street until, at last, a shanty housing complex appeared. Its windows were dirty and garbage was strewn along the tiny private yard. It was clear this was one of the festering slum homes which housed dozens of people. No doubt Barachos didn't even have a room to himself; perhaps a corner, with a flea-bitten cot. Poor families crowded into these places, pooling together the money to pay for expenses. Living in Korthos was no cheap affair.

The rusty gate had a lock, but it had broken. Gaia opened it with ease and entered the garbage-filled yard. In front of her, two boys were playing with terracotta soldiers. The people living here were the dregs of the city. The wealthy and well connected where Gaia lived, on Jewelers Row, considered these the refuse of the earth. But seeing these two children, pale and gaunt, Gaia felt compassion stirring in her heart. Was it their fault they were born to parents, stupid or unlucky? Their hearts beat just like hers; they breathed, they drank, they ate. She and her peers had been too dismissive of them.

They did not turn to look as she walked past.

Rickety wooden stairs led up to the living quarters of this shanty house. The smell of mildew and dust became apparent as she entered and opened the scratched, unlockable door.

In a grim hall—composed of tile, but chipped and stained with mud—there were doors with numbers. Records said Barachos lived in the one marked "Three."

Barachos had not paid his taxes in years. But Gaia did not intend to bring the topic up.

She sought knowledge. She did not even intend to take his book—only page through it, and then only if he allowed it.

She knocked on the door. There was some noise from beyond, some rustling and some footsteps. Perhaps Barachos would not show his face at all.

There were footsteps; the door cracked open, and a face appeared.

He was dusky, a southron if Gaia had ever seen one. His skin was an ochre red, his eyes dark yet bright. He was thin, yet his presence was imposing. Gaia wondered if she was looking at a sorcerer.

There was surprise in those dark eyes. Why was a rich woman speaking to him, he might wonder. Perhaps Gaia should have dressed in plainer clothes.

"What do you want?" he said. His accent was thick.

When Gaia told him she sought "The Ancient Ones of Stygia," and offered to pay him twenty *doukon*—twice the price he had paid—he refused.

Instead, a smile grew on his face. "I will not defraud a

fellow seeker…"

Inside Barachos' apartment, there were stone fetishes and idols in makeshift alcoves. On a table in one room was the book Gaia sought. It was a scroll, with yellowed and cracked parchment. It was clear "The Ancient Ones of Stygia" was written long ago.

"Do you seek knowledge of the demiurge?" asked Barachos.

Without answering, Gaia unraveled the scroll and found its length much greater than she anticipated.

It was written in Classical Eloesian, which she could read, with exceptional difficulty.

"The Ancient Ones of Stygia" was a hymn.

The hymn offered praise to one god after another. The Classical Eloesian was replete with words Gaia did not understand. She had to scan to the bottom of the scroll to find what she was looking for.

TO THE DEMIORGOS, IMPRISONED IN…

The words at that point became illegible.

WHO FORGETH THE WEAPONS IN THE FLAME…
WITH THY HAND THOU POINT, AND SEAL A SOUL
UNTO THY OWN…
AND HE WHOM THOU SEALEST CAN NEVER
BREAK THE BOND…

AND HE WHO IS SEALED SHALL COME TO THY
MOUNTAIN ON BENDED KNEE…
THE MOUNTAINS SHALL SHOUT, THY SERVANTS
SHALL WAR… THE CHAINED ONE SHALL BREAK

HIS CHAINS… THE PEOPLE WLL KNOW HE IS GOD…

Had she been sealed by this dark god's hand? And how could a god be imprisoned? How could the "Demiorgos" be restrained? And if he was restrained, could someone free him?

Gaia looked up to Barachos and saw, no longer, a hospitable stranger, but an evil man.

A chain was wrapped around his bicep. In his other hand, he had fetched another chain, which he was offering to her. "Until the master is freed… we will all be bound. Every one of us who follows him."

Gaia backed away in disgust. "How do I free myself? How do I break away from the bond?"

"He whom the true god sealeth can never be unsealed… to him who has a bond with him, he is bound in eternal chains."

She grabbed the chain from his hand. She threw it out the window. She spat on Barachos and fled the home in a fury.

But the dreams would continue. The haunting would endure. The demiurge had sealed her; and what bond he forged, no human could break.

SOMEWHERE IN THENOA

It was with a heavy heart that Hyron pursued this mission.

A hundred hoplites walked with him, together with a dozen cavalry. They intended to kill Theron, hero of the Southron War; but Hyron intended to capture him instead, and beg for Kunar's mercy on his behalf.

He could not see his friend killed, even if Kunar's anger had been stirred up by the Mount of Prophecy.

The terrain they traveled was barren and desolate; pines clung to ill-favored soil; in places the earth was cracked for lack of rain. Here they were, in the region once called Stygia, and Mount Tharnos was in view.

In size, Mount Tharnos could not compare to the peaks just outside Thénai, but climbing it would be daunting for a man of Hyron's age. Its outline against the blue sky was red rock and dark green; from the base to the summit it was covered in cypresses.

Here, according to the mad utterings of the Oracle, Theron was; and with him, the one she called his "teacher."

It would be difficult to stop the hoplites from following Kunar's orders; they would set upon Theron quickly. They would cut him down without flinching; and Hyron would have to exert great effort to restrain them. But it was worth it for his old friend—Theron, hero of the Southron War.

~

The sun beat hot on the mountainside, but Hyron and his men—some in full armor—continued through their exhaustion, duty-bound by Kunar's command. Again and again Hyron asked them to stop; and no amount of water could quench his thirst. He was too old for this. He was too old for this exertion, this risk.

But he was the leader of the Thenoan League; the nation had placed his absolute trust in him. Kunar—having given him all power—was relying on him as well. Could he put the Thenoan League above all his feelings? Could he betray his friend, on behalf of his loyalties?

Again they stopped beside a babbling brook which turned, yards away, into a waterfall gushing down the mountainside. There was one path here, one path which led to the mountain's summit.

There was little information gathered; most soldiers and the guides he had brought along with them believed he would be somewhere near the top.

Theron was clearly hiding; he knew the danger he was in, but how? Who had told him King Kunar was out for blood? Who told him that Hyron—once his closest friend—had betrayed him, throwing his lot in with those who sought to take Theron's life?

The sun's intensity was even worse, this high up. Hyron's tunic was drenched with sweat. He questioned whether he could go on. Pensively he walked up to the water's edge; he cupped the freezing-cold water in his hands and slurped it down. His knees ached, and pain was flaring up in places he never thought possible. He wanted nothing more than to be back home, in the city where he had lived all his life; but his duty demanded this—this misery.

"Look!" one of the guides shouted.

He was pointing to something in the distance.

"What is it?" a soldier said.

The guide led them all up the steep incline.

"I don't know," the guide said. "Something is off…"

There were no footprints to be seen. If anyone had passed by, the last week's rain had washed all traces away. But this guide knew the wilderness. He could tell if something was disturbed; if someone or something had passed through.

Soon the guide was gone. Disguised by his brown-and-green clothing, he had vanished into the landscape.

"Andros!" another guide shouted. Then, quieter, he murmured, "He's gone…"

Again Hyron turned to the water's edge. Thirsty and overheated, the water refreshed him more than fine wine. It was a shame they only had dry roadbread and salted meat to feed themselves; and in the best of circumstances, this mission would take several days.

He was, truly, too old for this.

An hour dragged on and the guide did not return. The sun had become oppressive in its intensity. It would not relent. And there was no relief coming; the sky was cloudless, and rain had not fallen in days.

The annoyance of soldiers at the guide's long absence turned to worried expressions and nervous talk.

What had happened to him? Was there a lion on this mountain, scouring for prey? Had Theron been eaten?

A hundred hoplites could surely take down a lion; but a guide, by himself, stood no chance against the king of beasts.

The commander of the hoplites approached Hyron. "I'm sending a few men to search…"

As he spoke, three hoplites were making their way up the steep incline. Hyron said a prayer for their souls… but his prior appeals to the gods had gotten him nowhere.

~

The sun was setting when the hoplites returned, rushing down the hill. "There is a lion… It must have taken Andros…"

When they described seeing its black mane and white fur, a

shudder went through Hyron's body. Were they prepared? In great numbers, the lion did not stand a chance. He prayed again, this time, that Amara would send poor Andros to the Fields of Paradise… and that she would protect Hyron and his men with her shield and spear.

He laughed at the thought of the "Virgin Queen of Battle," her ridiculous shield and spear, her golden image which once stood in her temple—before it was pilfered and turned over to Isteroi gods.

The fellow guides were fighting tears, but these were tough mountain men. They would continue their mission stoically. It was too bad a life was lost.

At night they continued the way up the mountain, until well after the moon had risen and the stars shone in all their brilliance. They pitched their tents, aware that at any time, the lion could show its face. They determined two hoplites would stand guard at any time while everyone else slept.

Hyron slept uneasily. Dark dreams consumed him, nightmares of bloodshed and warfare, of a black hand forged of steel, of the collapse of the Thenoan League and the slaughter of thousands of innocents.

~

It was just moments after they resumed their journey, not long after dawn, when the hoplites at the front of the caravan began shouting in horror.

Strung to a tree, dangling from a branch, was the bludgeoned head of the guide, severed clean from its neck. Flies were buzzing around the putrid flesh, and its eyes were frozen in the abject terror of death.

A lion had not killed Andros. A man had. But who?

SOMEWHERE IN THEMURIA

Snow was falling, a bitter wind was blasting down through the valley, and each day dozens of Rogon's soldiers died. At last count, a week ago, only seven-thousand soldiers remained alive and more were deathly ill; some had been taken with frostbite, and others—afflicted with gangrene—were forced to remove their limbs.

The soles of their shoes had begun to wear; misery was the rule of the day. Certain death was overtaking them, and few expected to make it back to the lowlands.

But Rogon continued on, filling them with false hope as best he knew how. But there were limits to his persuasion, and when even he had become convinced of their ultimate death, he proved a poor messenger.

The snow had reached depths Rogon had never imagined. Markers led the way along the road, but a few more inches and even they would be covered, forever obscuring the path out.

One by one they died. One by one the winter claimed them. They had butchered so many horses for food, hardly a one remained. As the days continued on, with no indication of how far they had to go, Rogon—whose optimism usually never faltered—began to lose hope.

The words of the Oracle continued to haunt him.

The Oracle told him to abandon his mission, to pursue his most hated enemy—Theron—and surrender his plans to destroy the Thenoan League. He would not follow her advice.

First he would conquer Eloesus, and deliver it to the southrons; then he would take his revenge.

The defeat on the Fields of Maratha still stung him. But one day soon, he would have Theron's head.

There were things to do first. There were worlds to conquer—all if, nameless god willing, he survived this journey.

BEDROOM, THE HOUSE OF THE SATYR, KORTHOS

Gaia woke up in a panic and tried to sit up, but found herself paralyzed. She could not move, and as she lay there, rigid as a statue, unmoving, breath turning to fog in the cold air, she knew the worst of nightmares was about to begin.

She could sense the demiurge before she saw him. She lay frozen, heart exploding in her chest, as she viewed the open door to her bedroom. Long before the sinewy black shape appeared, she could feel the creeping dread of his presence.

Tall and slender, the shadow appeared—a silhouette in the shape of an armored man. Its red eyes, like beacons, were looking into hers.

A chill set over her, but she was voiceless. Her mouth would not move. She could not speak. She could not scream.

And yet the demiurge slithered up to her and loomed over her on her bed.

"What dost thou seek above all else, Gaia daughter of Andromedion?"

Gaia felt like she was in a prison, in a hell of her own making. Suddenly, she gasped for air. She could speak. She could scream. But she did not scream. She cried, "Please leave me be… Leave me, demiurge… free me…"

Instantly she froze up again, unable to speak, unable to scream. The demiurge loomed over her; his pitch-black hands were just inches from her flesh. She wanted to weep for fear, but she was immobile.

"Freedom comes at a price…

"And the price I require will benefit thee greatly… for I know what thou sleekest above all else, Gaia daughter of

Andromedion… It is power that thou sleekest… power to change the world… power to shape the world in thy image… power which man doth not happily give to women."

What she truly sought was to be free of this curse. Every night she feared going to sleep. She worried each night that this very nightmare would happen. She was in a hell of her own design. She had called forth the Portal, all in hopes of regaining influence in the Assembly; and instead she was drawn ever deeper into a waking nightmare.

"Go, Gaia daughter of Andromedion… Go to the mount called Kronos… and in its caverns you will find my Gauntlet, forged of steel. To him who wears the Gauntlet of the Demiurge, endless power will be given to him… power which can remake nations and shake the very earth.

"Seek after my Gauntlet, and I shall not haunt your dreams… to the mount called Kronos, go…"

MOUNT THARNOS SUMMIT

Three days' journey, an arduous climb, and what had it gotten them? A death of a guide, a dwindling food supply, drained energy and damage to Hyron's knees which he doubted he'd ever recover from.

Theron was nowhere to be seen. The Oracle was proved, finally and totally, to be a madwoman devoid of knowledge. The hero of the Southron War, whom King Kunar was so eager to kill, was nowhere to be found.

Theron's life might be preserved. And yet Hyron was not relieved. In fact, he was disappointed he'd come back to Thénai empty handed, after all this effort, after all this exhaustion. Hyron, an old man, would not recover from this toilsome climb, this wasted effort.

A loud galloping sound encircled them. A horn blew. Out of the brush emerged a horse-rider with a javelin; he tossed it, impaling the commander of the hoplites, and drew his bow.

This was no horse-rider. From the top up he looked human; from the bottom down he was horse.

Was this a centaur, like the legends spoke of, or was Hyron deluded?

While hoplites charged—futilely, for the centaur easily outran them—or fled away altogether into the wilderness, Hyron merely froze up, paralyzed in indecision.

The centaur was shooting arrows as he galloped this way, then that. One by one hoplites fell to his arrows. Then, out of the brush, came a roaring lion.

No, this was not a lion, but Theron himself, donned in a lion-skin. In his right hand was a club; in his left a stone.

He threw the stone so hard it cracked a hoplite's helmet and sent him flying to the ground in a pool of blood.

As his friend the centaur picked off the rest, Theron charged the hoplites and slew them one after the other, beating them savagely with his club.

Hyron could not bring himself to run. Running would do him no good. He watched as the hoplites and guides, men he had come to know, were beaten down or slain by the centaur's arrows.

Hyron turned, seeking an avenue to escape, but the centaur was circling around them among the field of bruised and bleeding hoplites. As Theron savaged the remaining survivors, the centaur—having recovered his spear—had begun stabbing the wounded.

When Hyron turned to face his old friend, Theron—covered in blood—was running toward him, eyes full of rage. "Traitor!" he was shouting. "Traitor!"

Two swift blows to the head, and Hyron collapsed. As he began to bleed to death, he mourned his decision. He cursed Kunar, the illegitimate king; and he cursed himself, for obeying him.

SOMEWHERE IN THEMURIA

The snow was whirling, the wind was blasting, and Rogon had begun to succumb to the cold.

Six thousand men remained alive; every last pack animal had been butchered for meat. With dozens dying every day, they had run out of food. The nagging doubt and fear had been replaced by Rogon's absolute certainty of their incoming death.

It had been weeks since they departed Arkadion, and it seemed they were no closer to their goal.

Then one day, as night neared, a wall of ice and snow appeared, one which they could not overcome. Rogon despaired and beat his hands against his chest. He cried out for the nameless god. He fell to his knees and gave up hope.

Months of snow and ice had piled this monstrous barrier together. He had led his men to certain death. He cursed his foolishness. How had he ever expected success? Winters were too harsh. The cold would claim them all, and it was all his fault.

A hand jerked him from his stupor.

He saw the face of a young man he had gotten to know, Kalemnon. The clouds had broken and the sun was shining on Kalemnon's face. The snow was white and sparkling.

"I believe in you," said Kalemnon. "You can get us out of this mess."

Rogon stood up. He drank the remnants of his waterskin. Though hungry and frail, he turned to see the thousands who still remained.

They were gaunt; their tunics were wet and tattered. They seemed—in many cases—at the precipice of death. Their horse-skins and furs could not fully take away the winter's chill. To flatlanders accustomed to warmth and comfort, a Themurian winter was graver than the worst of battle wounds.

Rogon turned his gaze to the giant snow-drift. He became focused on the brilliant blue sky and the sun—a burning, fiery orb which gave light to the world.

Fire would be their salvation. As a student of the magi who stole secrets from the Grand Fire Temple, Rogon knew everything there was to know about fire.

And fire could save them.

He turned again to Kalemnon. "Get me as much wood as you can find."

And trees were abundant. In his pockets, he had quicklime and saltpeter and a half-finger of Theranian powder. If he could recall the method—and if his frigid, strained hands could mix the fire properly—he might prevail.

When the bundle of sticks had been brought to him, and when he had mashed the quicklime, saltpeter and Theranian powder in a mortar and pestle, he was aware of the precarious danger he had found himself in. The fire he was about to conjure was worthy of this wall of ice and snow; it could also, if handled improperly, kill them all.

He set the sticks against the edge of the snow-drift and carefully layered the silvery powder onto the twigs. Then, with a flint and tinder, he cast sparks on to the bundle, and—as anticipated—the furious fire burst into life.

Within moments, the inferno was blazing twice Rogon's height, and though he staggered backwards the intense heat nearly burned him. Snow quickly turned to puddles of water, revealing dead grass and leaves beneath.

The massive snow drift began to disintegrate, and water replaced it, washing down the mountainside.

When the fire had finally burned itself out, the snow-drift was gone, and there—beyond the puddles of water—the road took a sudden turn downward into the valley below.

The path was open. They would prevail.

Six-thousand soldiers would march into Thenoa unexpected and unannounced. Thanks to fire and bravery and the nameless god, Rogon's plans would succeed—as had all his other plans before.

FALSEHOOD

For months the student had sought the diploma—which his parents called a "worthless piece of parchment"—and already he was running into trouble.

His goal was slipping away. All because he could not answer, "What is truth?"

MOUNT THARNOS SUMMIT, THENOA

One-hundred and three bodies lay before Theron. He had counted them, one after the other, while Aigon scoured the mountain for enemies.

One twitching, bloodied body he recognized from his former life.

Hyron had been a friend. But he was a friend no longer; he had joined forces with those who sought to kill him. He had become a pawn of the Mount of Prophecy.

Bloodied and exposed to the sun, Hyron was still wheezing.

Theron struck him again and crushed his skull.

It was still, to a large extent, a mystery why the Oracle had turned against him. Not even Aigon knew… only that, toward the end of his life, the hero Phillipidēs faced the same enemy.

Aigon, six hundred years old, the last of the centaurs, had hid on this mountain and watched the life-ages of mankind pass by.

Out of the brush, Aigon came galloping, bow in hand. "I don't see anyone," said Aigon. "But we have to go. We've been compromised. They know where you are."

But where would they go?

It did not matter, for now. Theron hurried down along the path, from the summit, toward the flatlands.

~

It was late afternoon when they reached the lowlands. Cypress-covered hills and snowy mountains lay in the distance. The world was quiet and still. Except for the songs of birds, no noise greeted them. The air was still.

Then, in the distance, there came the sound of galloping. A woman was riding away, dressed in a blue hooded gown. This was a Maid of the Mount of Prophecy. Theron took off at a sprint and Aigon thundered ahead.

But, as the sun set, the woman began to pull ahead of them, and Aigon slowed his gait. Eventually his breakneck gallop turned to a trot. They would lose her.

Aigon turned to Theron, who had stopped in exhaustion.

"We can track her," he said.

Aigon had survived so long in the wilderness that he had become a master of it. There was no doubting the truth of Aigon's words.

But was all this effort worth it?

Theron had learned to trust Aigon's judgment. He had counseled him over these weeks, given him vast knowledge of the world and of Theron's place in it. Aigon, the ancient tutor of heroes, always knew which path to take.

KORTHICA, OUTSIDE MOUNT KRONOS

A day's journey along the road, and Gaia—though riding in a carriage and pampered by her servants—felt something like exhaustion when she arrived.

Mount Kronos had erupted years ago, wiping out ancient towns and burying them with dark silt. Now, vineyards were springing up, and farmers—lured by the cheap land—were building homes in the mountain's shadow. Industry was taking over, and as Gaia's carriage rattled across the road, there were barrels of wine fermenting outside farmers' homes, and other enterprising vintners sowing seeds.

Word had spread in Korthos that the soil in this region was astoundingly fertile. Out of the tragedy of the volcanic eruption, something good had emerged.

But though Gaia's nightmares had ceased ever since agreeing to the demiurge's request, seeing the mountain and knowing of the task which had been placed upon her, she wondered if she had made the right decision.

The monstrous being which plagued her dreams had demanded his so-called "Gauntlet" as a price for freeing his control. But the jagged mountain, black and red, was as foreboding as it had been in the days before the eruption: in fact, even now, smoke was rising from the summit.

Even with her servants, a woman such as Gaia seemed ill fit to the task.

The sun had begun to set in golds and reds when the carriage halted its journey. Close to the mountain, a lone inn had been built. Some homes surrounded it, and a makeshift market—the beginnings of a town.

Gaia's servants helped her out of the carriage, then led it around the corner to the stables.

A charmed life, she lived—but she had not always been so lucky. As a girl, her parents did not have the means to afford a servant. Everything had to be done by themselves, by hand.

Another servant left to negotiate with the innkeeper inside while others unloaded Gaia's luggage: chests containing clothing, cosmetics and personal items.

She turned to face the dreaded Mount Kronos. Its black, ash-colored slopes were bereft of any trees. Its dark shape formed a silhouette against the blue sky and sea around it. Somehow, Gaia would have to enter this forbidding mountain, and find what the demiurge sought. She had grave doubts she would survive the effort; but death seemed less a threat than the continuance of her nightmares.

And so, tomorrow morning, she would set about her task. Her servants did not know why they'd come here; she would not tell them. This mission was hers and hers alone.

THE HIGH ROAD, THENOA

From the heights of the mountains, Rogon and his six-thousand soldiers had descended to the warmth of the lowlands. The blighted snowy hell-scape had given way to the hills surrounding Thénai.

They were behind enemy lines, in the heart of Thenoan territory. Their enemies were unprepared.

Some hoplites had died of lingering sickness even after they reached the warmth of the lowlands. But those who remained were strong, and ready to fight.

The words of the Oracle were omnipresent. Go, she had told him, and kill Theron.

But such things could wait. The sack of Thénai, the devastation of the Thenoan League, would ensure eternal control over the Eloesian nation.

And then, when Rogon was vested with such incredible power, he could finally avenge his defeat on the Fields of Maratha—the humiliation which he had endured, but did not deserve.

It was ten days' long march until they reached Thénai, and that was in the best of circumstances. Surprised and unawares, the enemy would have no time to react.

The plans were in place. The Kersican Navy would blockade. Thénai would crumble.

Rogon would prevail.

CITY SQUARE, THÉNAI

Khloë, amazon, Eloesian citizen, and Theron's friend, had spent the darkest winter of her life within the city's bounds.

She still clung to hope that Theron was alive. A rumor had spread that he had survived the shipwreck.

But Khloë had seen who was after him. She had uncovered who wanted him dead. Theron had conquered the southrons, even Rogon, the Dark Captain, the Butcher of Nissos; but could he overcome the all-seeing Oracle, who knew all and saw all?

For now, she had stayed put in the safety of the city, in the safety of her own anonymity.

She had abandoned her allegiance to Korthos. For her loyalty, she had been awarded Thenoan citizenship. She had offered a sacrifice before the civic gods and been welcomed into the Thenoan community.

And the Thenoans, unlike the Korthians, had treated her as one of their own, for the most part. They made an effort to help Khloë feel welcome—that she was "one of them," even if she wasn't one of them.

The tumult of the prior months had brought her here, to the square. It was here she hoped to find information. In the corner of the squalid square, a fortune teller had set up shop.

The fortune teller, a southron, had a large silver bowl set out on the table. The bowl was filled with water. Near the bowl was a leaden cup half-filled with *doukon* and *thalon*. This southron had done well for himself by preying on the needs of the desperate: the desperate like Khloë.

With a small amount of nervousness, Khloë took her seat across from the fortune teller. Back home, in Amazonia, fortune tellers were scorned as frauds. But this was the desperation she had found herself in. She would not rest until she found Theron… dead or alive.

"What do you seek?" Only now did she see half of the fortune teller's face was covered in disfiguring scars; and on that side, his eye was goopy white. On the other side, the fortune teller was handsome and dusky, and his eye functioned perfectly.

"Where is my friend?" asked Khloë. "His name is…"

"Theron," the fortune teller answered.

Khloë's disbelief lasted only a few moments. This fortune teller was an expert gatherer of information. It was part of his allure. He of all people would know Khloë's closeness with Theron.

If she sought to find the truth, there was little chance this fortune teller would give it.

"Theron… I can see him. He is under the sea. He is dead…" The fortune teller was peering into the bowl of water.

But Khloë had a feeling. This fortune teller had to be wrong. She had a keen sense for things. If anyone could survive a shipwreck amid a stormy sea, her friend Theron could.

But what if it was true? If his body lay anywhere, it was in the deeps, fed-upon by sharks and abominations of the sea.

"Tell me, fortune teller, what happened to your eye?" The goopy white mass filled her with mixed pity and revulsion.

"I was a young boy. Pirates raided my island. They killed almost everyone in my village, but I managed to hide…" The gaze of his good eye unnerved Khloë so much she glanced away. "And when I emerged a day later… the sun was hot. Flesh flies were buzzing everywhere. They bit me all over. And weeks later, I looked into my reflection in a pond, and I saw this horror. The gods had forsaken me; and so I turned to magic. I regret nothing."

Despite the inaccuracy of her reading, Khloë placed two *thalon* in the cup. "Thank you," she said. As soon as she could, she fled from the fortune teller's gaze. She could not bear to look into the horror of those scars and that eye.

Khloë had taken up residence in a cramped upper-story room above a sandal-maker's shop. There she had stowed her most prized possessions; and from the odd-jobs she took up, she could just barely afford to pay her upkeep. All her spare time was spent searching for Theron, hoping against hope that he'd remember her, that he would find his way back... that he would consider Khloë important enough to return to.

She spent the rest of the day unloading jars of flour from a ship in the Thenoan harbor; and then, with just one *doukon* to show for her work, she bought herself a cupful of wine and a loaf of bread. Dusk was setting in when she returned to her makeshift home...

And the fortune teller was waiting there. She recoiled in horror at his scarred face, at the white eye, at the sun setting over his warped skin, his hooded cloak. "What are you doing?" cried Khloë. Her first instinct was to grab her sabers; but he posed no true threat to her. With exceptions—such as Theron—human men were weaker than amazons.

Still, the sight of him made her skin crawl.

"I said, what are you doing?" She sounded hysterical now. She was trembling.

"Do you know that Theron has a blood price? Whoever brings King Kunar Theron's head... he will be given twenty gold pieces."

"Get away from me," snarled Kloe. "Never come back here. Or I'll have your head."

She swept her sabers out and the fortune teller fled away, into the coming night.

That night she lit a candle by her window. She left her closet door open. Any shadow, any compartment, any nook could hide the monster who stalked her.

A pounding on her door woke her from her sleep. In a panic she imagined the fortune teller just outside. She grabbed her sabers. "Who is it?" she cried.

The candle by her window had blown out. The night was deep and dark; it was well before dawn.

"Who is it?" she cried again.

The door burst off its hinges. A hoplite—the one who kicked it in—entered bearing a sword and shield. Three more were behind him. "Our king would like a word with you," said the hoplite.

"And if I don't want to go?"

The hoplite gave a signal. They rough-handled her, cutting her belt and removing her sabers. One bound her hands behind her back.

"Come with us," he said.

As she walked outside the room, into the corridor, the fortune teller was standing there. He had sold her out. He had used the information she had given him, and betrayed her.

EDGE OF THENOA

Aigon had gathered the firewood. Theron had gone fishing.

Together, they had conspired to a night of enjoyment after many days in the wild.

The cicadas were singing, the stars were shining, and the forests hid Theron and Aigon from the world. Yet Aigon was tracking the Maid of Prophecy with ease, and was insistent that they would catch her eventually.

Theron's nets had caught them ten trout—more than he could comfortably eat. But Aigon, ever ravenous, would surely finish them off.

Out of twigs, Theron carved skewers and made a makeshift grill. He gutted and filleted the fish and then set them to cooking. In the fire's glow, the grease dripped off the crispy scales, and after days of eating dry road bread, Theron couldn't bear to wait.

But then Aigon looked backwards, into the darkness of the woods. "Do you hear that?"

Theron saw on Aigon's face something he had never witnessed before: fear.

For a moment Theron stood up from his cooking. He had lost interest in food. "What is it?"

Aigon's pointed ears perked up. He backed away from the fire and grabbed his bow. "Hush," he said. "Come with me."

Aigon took off at a trot and Theron sprinted after him, leaving the cookware behind. The trout could burn, for all he cared.

Theron had reached his limits when Aigon came to a sudden halt. They had to have run four miles in total. Panting and sweating, Theron steadied himself.

Through a veil of leaves and bushes, there were torches.

Soldiers were marching through the wilderness… hundreds. No, thousands.

These were not Thenoans.

There were Kersicans, there were Kersepolans. There were southron auxiliaries in turbans and Ten Cities men in Megarine caps. Their number stretched into the distance.

Had they truly come from Themuria? Had they marched through that barren land in winter? It verged on impossible. How could so many soldiers survive the ice and snow?

The sound of their marching feet shook the leaves and the trees.

Theron ran ahead, and beyond the countless ranks, he could see the insectoid helmet of black iron.

Somehow, despite all odds, the Dark Captain had survived.

He should have killed Rogon while he had a chance. He should have slain him on the Field of Maratha. But he had not. He had been too merciful.

The old Theron would have let him go. The new Theron would have cut him down and let crows feast on his flesh.

But he was not a fool. Even Theron, who slew the Carceran Lion, could not defeat all these thousands of soldiers.

He felt the presence of Aigon looming behind him.

"You know him."

Theron nodded.

"They are headed towards Stygia…"

"Toward Thénai," Theron corrected him. Aigon had an old-fashioned sense of geography—no, an archaic one.

But here they were, at a decision point.

The Thenoan side of him said to follow this army. The Eloesian, the citizen within him told him to follow Rogon and his horde.

But the side of him which Aigon saw—the hero—told him

to pursue the Mount of Prophecy… to force her to spill the truth of why the Oracle had turned against him.

"Let's go," Aigon said. His gaze was turned to the mountains. The Oracle was who he sought.

But Theron lifted up his hand, and Aigon paused.

"We are following the army…"

"To Stygia?"

When Theron made up his mind, not even Aigon could convince him otherwise.

WAYFARERS INN, KORTHICA

Early in the morning, Gaia arose. Her servants had prepared her a bath in the courtyard; and with a hunk of lye soap, she washed herself down to prepare for the day—a day which her servants had no idea of.

Back in her chamber, she picked out the clothes she cared about the least: a yellow gown which, despite its status as her cheapest raiment, would be considered fabulously expensive by a commoner; and a hood which she fastened around her head. She had brought a dozen pairs of shoes, some for walking, some for dancing, some for impressing; but she chose a pair of ruddy leather loafers which were dispensable.

In the main hall of Wayfarers Inn, her servants had already taken it upon themselves to order food: fruit and sweet cream, pine nuts and fresh white cheese. She only ate a small portion of the platter before her, washing it down with wine.

She had to admit, she was nervous. To find the demiurge's so-called gauntlet in Mount Kronos… how could she begin this strange quest that had been set before her?

But she would go.

And so, after she had filled her stomach, she left the warmth of the inn, headed out to the stables, and mounted a painted horse named Magala. With the help of a servant, she left the fenced-in enclosure, and—with a cluck of her tongue—took off at a trot toward the baleful black mountain.

~

From a distance, the jagged mountain looked black; but

now, up close, its color was ash-gray. The air was dusty and thick. Along the bleak slopes, wilted black trees clung to life.

And though Gaia saw no creature stirring, she felt like she was being watched.

No life could survive in this accursed place.

But she had become convinced she was not alone.

She led sweet Magala up to one of the wilted black trees. She dismounted and fastened her to one of its spindly branches.

Then, still quaking, she drew in a deep breath and decided to continue her climb.

She slipped on the loose rock and fell on her face.

She pushed herself up with sore, reddened hands.

She was not meant for this.

She had donned her cheapest, most tight-fitting shoes, but even they were meant for luxury.

Her gown almost tripped her when she took another step.

And she had so much further to go before she reached the summit.

She wished she had brought helpers. But what would they think?

Her servants were not immune to spreading gossip about their mistress. If she told her servants what she was doing—seeking after a supposed "Gauntlet" which she was told about in a dream—word would spread across Korthos that she was insane.

But this was real. She was sure of it.

Hoisting her gown up, Gaia continued up the unsteady path, and made it only a yard before she slipped again.

She did not fall this time.

Still, she cursed.

She removed her shoes and found the rocky slope was

pleasantly warm. The pebbles grated on her toes, but her footing was sure.

From her pocket, she grabbed a knife, and proceeded to cut the gown until it was above her knee. It wouldn't get in her way anymore.

And she did not put her knife back in her pocket. She could still feel those eyes watching her; and every time a wind rustled across the slopes, it seemed Mount Kronos had come alive.

~

She had never exerted herself to this extent. Her hair had become wet with sweat; she had discarded her hood. Her hands had become grimy. She was panting and out of breath.

As she drew closer to the summit, the heat of the rocky slope and of the air had grown more intense. She had broken a branch off one of those sickly trees, and used it as a walking stick; but the climb still taxed her to her limits.

When, at last, she came within striking distance of the bubbling fire of the summit, the exhaustion came to a fore, and she collapsed.

She drank what was left in her water-skin.

She missed the comforts of home. What she wouldn't give to be back in Korthos, in her comfortable home, with a glass of red wine, in her nightclothes.

She could see the splendid city from here, on the roof of the world. Its form was hazy, but clearly evident, built along the sparkling shores of the sea. It was far-gone now, as distant as a dream. Would she ever return? She had her doubts.

In the shadow of the mountain, death seemed to be pressing in on her; but if death came, she would be relinquished of the nightmares.

The remainder of her water failed to slake her thirst. The mountainside was dry and barren, with no ponds or brooks running down. How good it would be to drink from an ice cold brook.

But it was not to be. Her fingers and arms were stained with the mountain's ash. She doubted that, in her entire life's span, she had ever been this dirty. Even growing up in a middling, not-altogether-wealthy household, Gaia's mother had impressed upon her that she should look her best. What would she say now?—gods rest her soul.

When she had caught her breath, she stood up and instantly stumbled. The mountain quaked. Out of the depths, a jet of fire shot from the caldera up ahead.

She said a prayer of protection to gods which she did not believe in; then she walked ahead, toward the flame, toward the fate which destiny had foisted upon her.

~

A drop-off led to the uneven floor surrounding the caldera. Many fathoms below, liquid fire still bubbled and boiled, and smoke arose.

The heat was so intense Gaia could scarcely breathe. It felt like her skin was burning.

She was coughing because of the smoke. She turned back, declaring her quest useless—a failure.

And above the bubbling and boiling of the fire, a noise arose—footsteps.

When she turned, she saw that a creature had appeared before her, standing just yards away along the caldera's rim.

She brandished her knife.

The creature was short and humpbacked, with a bushy brown mane. Its eyes were yellow and crazed.

Gaia screamed, dropped her knife and fled.

She ran right into the arms of a creature just like it.

She backed away and shrieked.

The creature held up its bulging, yellow-nailed thumb. He pushed it up to her lip. "Hush," the creature said.

"*Yaga yaga Kroniod!*" a voice said from behind her. "*Demiorgos!*"

These monsters did not intend to kill her. Someway, somehow, they had knowledge of her plans. These were the despicable servants of the demiurge.

The two creatures scurried ahead of her and—despite the searing heat and choking smoke, Gaia followed after them. As the caldera bubbled and boiled below her, the creatures led her down into a crevasse and into total darkness.

~

The darkness was refreshingly cool, and as the crevasse quickly turned into a steep drop-off, the relief from the heat banished fear from her mind.

Amid her rapid descent into the mountain's heart, illumination steadily grew until the darkness was partially erased, revealing tunnels that—far from crude and natural—were carved by chisel, in perfect angles, even ornamented with patterns. Light was filtering in from small windows which faced the caldera, even as the sharply-descending tunnels went further into the mountain depths.

Flashes of light from the mountain's boiling fire illuminated images carved along the tunnels: pictures of creatures, just like the ones in front of Gaia, waging war against human soldiers. Ye the flashing lights illuminated the strange armor which they wore, and great engines of the Old Dominion which they used to blast their enemies.

Gaia, running and stumbling downward in a frenzy, as fast as she could go, was still falling behind the creatures. They were pulling ahead of her; and she would be alone.

She took off at a sprint and hit the ground hard, scratching her knees against the flagstone floor.

The creatures were gone.

Unarmed and unprotected, she was easy prey for whatever horrors inhabited this mountain labyrinth.

It had become clear that the demiurge was merely a title of Kronos. The demon who haunted Eloesus in ancient days had another name.

But why did the texts talk of the demiurge, chained and banished into a prison?

Gaia thought that, perhaps, there was more to Kronos than anyone else knew.

Weeping from the pain, Gaia stood up and continued her journey at an easy pace. Without a guide, there was no point in exerting herself. She would find her way to the mountain's depths, or she would perish. Either way, she wouldn't run there.

~

Soon the tunnel had taken her beneath the bubbling fire.

Total darkness greeted Gaia.

These creatures which lived in the mountain could—perhaps—see in the dark.

Now she was cautious, walking slowly, stepping gingerly over the flagstone to make sure she didn't trip.

Though she could not see, the tunnel only led one way:

swiftly downward, into the mountain's heart.

As Gaia gained her footing, despite the deep darkness, she increased her speed. Eventually her descent had turned almost to a fall as she navigated the swiftly-dropping tunnel.

Then she hit a wall. She cursed at the unforeseen obstacle. She touched her bruised cheek and felt blood. She grasped around in the darkness, finding nothing, no wall, no corridor.

Then, the sound of a hammer striking metal echoed through the air. She followed and found herself a new direction, a new tunnel to navigate.

With one hand on a sturdy wall, she continued her downward journey, through the swiftly-descending tunnel.

The beating of the hammer continued to echo, and then the jabber of the creatures ahead.

Somehow, she had caught up to them.

The corridor took a steep downward turn. Gaia almost fell as she quickened her descent into the mountain's heart.

The sound of the hammering was growing more and more audible, echoing through the tunnels. Light had begun to filter in, and out of the corner of her eyes, Gaia could see more creatures hiding in crevices and lurking near hallways, their eyes glinting green in the dimness.

She had no time for terror or panicking; the swiftly-dropping tunnel was forcing her onward, whether she liked it or not. Her feet were bruising after all this walking, but so great was her determination to end her nightmares, she did not hesitate.

She hit a wall and staggered back, stunned, to the sound of the creatures laughing. There were dozens of them now, perhaps a hundred, following her inept journey through the darkness.

The light strengthened, and once more the rabbit's warren of tunnels were illuminated with a red glow. The reliefs of subterranean creatures carved along the walls formed a narrative:

bat-like monsters with skeletal heads; squid-like creatures dragging themselves into battle; and winged skulls breathing fire. Whoever had carved these tunnels was clearly mad, yet very skilled—more skilled than these dim-witted creatures could be. The hand that etched these faces, these claws, these strange appendages, was masterful—as masterful as the sculptors in Korthos.

Masterful, the artwork was—but demented.

The cool of the subterranean tunnels began to fade, and as the light intensified—peeking in through slits in the walls—the warmth intensified also.

As the visibility increased, the creatures who had been watching her and laughing at her struggles scurried away. These creatures, which dwelled deep beneath the earth, were afraid of an unarmed woman. She had come to believe they were cowardly; and whichever master they served, they were poor servants.

A bubbling and boiling became audible against the steady strike of the hammer. The fire of the mountain's heart was nearby. At last another corridor opened up, a tunnel which ran from side to side. At the end of it, she could make out a vault—and beneath it, bubbling and boiling flame.

She did not know why, but she was certain the Gauntlet of the Demiurge lay somewhere ahead.

The tunnel opened up to another chasm. Down a steep drop was a lake of boiling fire which burst and bubbled and steamed beneath her. Beyond the corridor, the ground spiraled downward at an even angle, circling the pit of fire. This, too, had been carved by a masterful hand.

Sensing the presence of the foul creatures behind her, she nonetheless continued where her heart told her to go—downward, to the lake of fire.

As it bubbled and crackled and spat up flame, she turned her eyes to its center and saw an island crafted of stone. In the center was an anvil… and striking it with a hammer was the source of the noise.

~

The demiurge's Gauntlet appeared to be suspended in the air. Gaia froze in place. She could see a faint tendril of black smoke exiting the Gauntlet—the vestigial hand of the demiurge, whom she had seen in her dream. All that could be seen of his arm in the material world was the black smoke filling the Gauntlet, billowing and then dissipating to nothing. This smoke was visible to the eye, but the physical world had no claim to it; this was merely a remnant of the demiurge's ancient presence, a vestige of when he walked the earth and forged vile weapons in the depth of the mountain.

And here it lay: the Gauntlet, hammering the anvil uselessly, doing what as its wearer had hundreds of thousands of years ago. Up above the chasm, the hairy creatures stalking her were emerging from caverns and holes, beside themselves with glee as Gaia approached her goal.

The heat was so intense, Gaia felt her skin was burning. Her hands were covered in soot. She could scarcely breathe. Yet she continued on, circling the bubbling and boiling cauldron of fire and then, at last, found herself just yards from the island.

The mountain shook and Gaia hit the black stone, just inches from the searing fire.

This mountain was unsteady; at any point the ground could shift and the stone cavern collapse in on her.

Coughing from the soot, she stood up once more, fearing the next quake could send her hurtling into the fire.

There was no easy path to the island. Rocks led the way—

jutting out from the lake of fire, they provided an unsteady bridge.

Did Gaia truly have the gumption?

She was not meant for this. She was a politician, a diplomat, a woman of the city. This journey had taken more strength from her than anything she'd done before.

Weeping and trembling, she wedged her foot onto one of the stones and took a wide step onto another. "Gods…" She never should have come. She should have let the nightmares continue until they killed her.

Fearing the mountain would quake again and send her into the bubbling fire, she continued lurching ahead, stone by stone, until at last her bare feet set foot on the island.

The Gauntlet was still striking the anvil with its hammer. Gaia walked up and grabbed a hold of it; the metal was icy to the touch. The hammer fell, ringing, to the ground. The black some wafted away, and the Gauntlet stopped its moving.

Above her, in the caverns and holes, the creatures were cheering and leaping up and down.

Gaia, somehow, had done an evil thing—but she didn't know what.

Near the anvil, along the edge of the island, there were discarded arms and armor—swords, helmets and shields which had never been worn. Many had rusted away. The work of the demiurge, Kronos, who had forged all these wonders in ancient times, had not been put to use.

Clutching the ice-cold Gauntlet in both hands, Gaia struggled across the makeshift bridge of stones.

The hairy creatures were leaping down from the heights to meet her on the other side. Excitement had overtaken their yellow-eyed, hairy-maned faces. They began motioning to her; and it became apparent they would lead her out of the mountain. Like the master who ruled over them, they wanted Gaia to take the Gauntlet into the outside world.

~

Through the shadows, up and down deep tunnels, and into pitch blackness for what seemed like days, Gaia followed her crazed guides.

At some point, when she had given up all hope of ever reaching her destination, they stopped and shoved aside a piece of wood.

The light filtering through illuminated a cellar. Racks of wine filled the room; a stairway led up into the upper floor.

She could hear the voices of her servants up above.

These creatures had carved tunnels all through this land; and no human habitation could prevent their coming and going. Gaia staggered ahead, and turned around to see the wooden panel shifting shut behind her.

She had survived. She had done as the demiurge wanted.

The nightmares would end.

But she was certain she had not heard the last of him.

A ROAD IN THENOA

They were still days from reaching the coast. Rogon had no doubts that the word had reached the cretins of the Thenoan League. The city of artists, philosophers and pederasts would break and buckle quickly under Rogon's effort. Having failed to foresee the winter crossing over the mountains, there were no preparations they could make. No fortress could bar their entry. Every village, every gold and silver mine, every shepherd's pasture, was Rogon's for the taking.

Yet despite the warmth and the pleasant weather, food had begun running low.

Hunger had returned to Rogon and his men had become famished.

When a path appeared, leading off the road toward a vast farm, Rogon knew just what to do.

He signaled his men to follow and led them away.

Farmhands sowing seeds in the fields turned and fled at the sight of Rogon.

"The Butcher! The Butcher!" one cried.

"The Butcher of Nissos!" screamed another.

In the distance, a shepherd took off at a sprint, and his flock of sheep stampeded after him.

An arrow stuck one of the farmhands in the back, and he collapsed.

Rogon laughed and turned, seeing one of his men had drawn a bow and shot the arrow. Another was drawing a bow to pick off the other. It had become a game.

So be it.

What worth did these farmers have that could give him

pause? Thenoans were pederasts, artists and sculptors. A nation as soft as they did not deserve to live.

A house lay ahead, and two silos no doubt full of grain. Cows wandered in a pasture beyond Rogon's sight. They would eat well tonight, once the bloodshed ended.

The farmer and his wife came running out of the house, intending to flee, but Rogon's men had surrounded him.

The woman fell to her knees and knit her fingers together, begging and weeping. The farmer dropped his knife and raised his hands in surrender.

Over the years, Rogon's men had become bloodthirsty. They would kill this couple and relish the fact.

Yet a part of Rogon did not want any harm to befall the crying woman.

He was the Butcher of Nissos; he had waged a vicious war, without any compunction, across the land.

And these farmers might tell the cities that they were coming. It was not prudent to let them live.

Yet Rogon lifted his hand. "Stop," he said. "Let them go."

"Thank you, thank you," the farmer's wife cried, and fled alongside her husband toward the outlying hills.

The soldiers who were eager for prey looked at Rogon askance and glared. Then grudgingly they enter the home to pilfer the valuables. Rogon doubted they'd find any.

But in the distance there were great barrels of wine fermenting; and out in the silo, soldiers were exiting with bags of grain. They would eat well.

At night, Rogon's men ate better than they'd ever eaten in Korthos. They butchered several cows and made cakes from the flour; they drank the half-fermented wine until there was not a drop left in the barrels.

Then, drunken and happy, one by one they fell asleep.

It was then, when everyone save the night watchmen had fallen asleep, that Rogon quietly exited the camp and made his way into the hills.

The wind blew from the east, making the wintry chill even harsher.

He marveled at what he had become.

He had not always been so callous, so merciless and so quick to kill.

As a young man, like a Rephathites, he had been trained with sword and bow. Yet he had been a sensitive soul. He had never wanted to take a life.

Yet when he—like all male Rephathites—enlisted in the King of Kings' army, he was of course called into war. It had grown easier and easier to take a life; and soon, not even the butchery he witnessed of rebellious towns fazed him.

Once, when he studied the art of fire-making with the magi on Mount Agni, one of the most senior of the magi had said something that cut deeply: "You are the most brutal, the most vicious warrior I have ever met."

He had not always been that way.

He had been innocent once… before he spilled first blood on the islands of Zubay… before he razed to the ground the rebellious village of Sharam-El, and sowed its fields with salt… before he pledged his heart and mind to the Nameless God, offering his blood before the idol.

He had not always been so callous, so vicious, so cruel.

But that is what he had become. That is who the Nameless

God had chosen him to be.

The wind was picking up strength, blowing in from the west, bone-chilling in its coldness, smelling of mountain flowers.

He turned and regarded a dark shape approaching.

His nightly commune with the Nameless God would have to wait.

A young woman was approaching him, struggling up the grassy hill in a gown which dropped to her ankles. She was clothed head to toe, in bright blue color, with a hood wrapped around her face. In her left hand was a walking stick. Far off in the distance, her horse could be seen, its breath turning to fog in the cold air.

He knew who this woman was, and what she represented. The eye of the so-called Mount of Prophecy had again turned to Rogon.

And the wind that blew, blew from Prophecy's bent peak.

It was amazing this woman was not afraid of Rogon, still wearing his iron helm, with his greatsword clipped to his side. Yet she approached him without fear.

She called out, "Rogon!"

The young woman could not be much older than sixteen. Someone once told Rogon that the Maids of Prophecy were sworn to lifelong virginity. She was beautiful. Would he cause her to break her oath?

"Rogon!" she cried, perhaps seeking acknowledgment— but he would not give her any. He just stared.

"I have an offer for you," she said. "An offer you can't refuse."

"I'm listening," Rogon answered.

"Theron has slipped away from our sight," said the Maid. "I don't think you understand the danger he poses."

"I will have his head," Rogon said, "in time."

"We must trap him," she answered. "And if you help us

snuff him out, my master will give you kingship over all Eloesus."

Rogon doubted the mad Oracle had such power. This woman had been following them for days, perhaps weeks, waiting for a chance to speak with Rogon privately. She would come up empty-handed.

"His power is growing," she said. "If we don't stop him, he will become impossible to defeat."

"I've vanquished much greater foes than Theron…"

And he would seize upon the so-called "hero of the Southron War"; he would have him burned alive as a sacrifice. But that could wait. He had great things to do, and much greater enemies to vanquish. He was on the cusp of the greatest victory of his life. No longer would he be feared and hated as the Butcher of Nissos, but the Butcher of Thénai. His name would live in the history books as Eloesus' most dreaded conqueror.

He turned and left. The hysterical Maid could go to her master and beg for forgiveness.

Slaying Theron would be easy.

For now, there were greater works to be done.

A ROAD IN THENOA

From their hiding place behind a tree, Theron and Aigon watched the Maid of Prophecy gallop across the hills.

Theron had picked up a large rock from the forest floor, intending to strike her down; but Aigon put his hand on Theron's and hissed, "Stop."

Theron had, more often than not, bucked Aigon's advice or disobeyed out of spite. But he had a sense of things. He could truly be putting himself in danger.

"If they see one of their own dead, they'll find us," Aigon said. "They'll know our trail. They'll know we're following the Korthians..."

They had kept far behind Rogon's party, fearing they'd be found out.

From a distance, Aigon tracked their trail of violence and destruction.

Days from the coast, in the desolate hill country, they had managed to create incredible butchery. Despite few living here save shepherds and the occasional homesteader, Theron and Aigon had witnessed much death and bloodshed; corpses bruised and battered, houses robbed and then set alight. Following behind Rogon was a trail of death. Wherever he went, destruction followed in his wake.

For the first time in a while, Theron consented to Aigon's advice. He dropped the stone he was holding. He watched as the Maid of Prophecy galloped into the distance, out of his grip, out of his sight. She would live—but only for now.

Once she was out of sight, Theron left the security of his hiding place and ventured out into the open. Hills stretched for miles around, brown mounds under a cloudy sky.

As Theron hurried ahead, bracing through the cold air, a

light drizzle began to fall.

How he hated winter.

~

Off the road, a house and a silo lay in smoldering ruins.

Two bodies lay rotting in the rain, bloated and buzzing with flies. Multiple arrows remained lodged in their flesh. Like barbarians, they had left these free Eloesians to rot in the open air; they had not buried their bodies and allowed them entry to the underworld.

"We must go," Aigon said.

This time Theron would not listen. He walked toward the burnt-out shell of a house.

After rummaging through the smoked-out ruins, seeing many bodies lying exposed in the fields, he caught sight of a silo which had not been touched.

~

After searching the entire farmstead, Theron eventually found a shovel lying in the fields. He walked out into the hills and began to dig a hole for the bodies.

Whether they lived on as shades in the gloomy river or entered the Fields of Paradise, it was not for Theron to decide. Only the gods knew what kinds of lives they lived, whether they were heroic and brave, and exceptional; or displeasing to the gods' sight.

Nonetheless, he picked a spot and—against the protests of Aigon—began to dig.

Some barbarians burned their dead, like the Fharese; others

piled them with stones, like the whiteskin nomads. An Eloesian deserved a burial, no matter how ignominious, no matter how immoral or greedy or cruel.

Despite the mud and the increasing rain, Theron dug until the pit was six feet deep. Aigon regarded him with glares throughout the entire hour; but when Theron was finished, muddy and miserable, he had no regrets.

He and Aigon dragged each body and tossed it in the pit; he counted seven lives taken by Rogon's animals.

When he had sealed the pit with dirt, he took a deep breath, and knew he'd done a good thing.

~

As he began to walk back toward the road, there was a loud scream. He turned to see a bloodied woman running toward him, clothed in rags.

It was clear she had been tortured. She was near death.

"Help! Help!" she screamed. She was hobbling. "My husband…"

"Show me where he is," Theron said, and followed her as she hobbled back in the other direction. Aigon followed close behind.

Across the hills, as a windstorm began and the rain fell, cold as ice, dropping in sheets from the sky; as the sun began to set and darkness to creep over the heavens; at last they found the woman's husband, bound and gagged, bearing clear evidence of torture.

These farmers had nothing to offer Rogon. He was so sadistic, he had tormented them for mere enjoyment.

Theron dropped his club and drew his hunting knife. He

knelt down beside the groaning man and gingerly cut his binds.

Aigon was not merely a centaur. He was a healer. If anyone could save these desperate people, Aigon could.

But would he? Knowing Aigon, he would consider this a waste of time, a distraction from the things that truly mattered.

But he also would do as Theron wished. He viewed Theron as his ward.

With a sigh, Aigon stooped down—awkwardly—with his horse-like legs. A bag was clipped to his belt, and from it he drew some thread and some knives.

Over the course of hours, he had wiped the blood from the man's body and fastened his wounds with cloth. He had knit his greatest wounds together with a needle and thread—something Theron had never seen before with Eloesian doctors. Then Aigon had propped him up and given him water, which Theron had drawn from the local well.

He and his wife would recover. But Aigon and Theron had lost a day. They had fallen far behind Rogon's army. In the end, Aigon's wisdom was correct. This had been a waste.

Were these lives worth saving, in the grand scheme of things? Would Thénai and all its holdings fall because Theron had insisted on a delay?

"I'll avenge you," Theron said. He had to move quickly. These farmers were in frail condition, but they would survive. Theron had no doubts about that.

"Thank you." His words were strained. He had lost a great deal of blood.

"Rogon—"

The farmer cut Theron off. "It was not the Dark Captain."

Even far from the coast, Rogon's dark deeds had become

legend.

"A woman…"

It could not be true.

"She said she sought Theron. She said he was wearing a 'lion-skin.' She thought he had come this way…"

Perhaps he was too dazed to see the lion-skin that Theron wore, or to comprehend it.

"Why?" Theron asked. "Why do they want to kill me?"

It was the farmer's wife who answered. "She said something… that you're disrupting something. She was not alone… She told her friend you are a 'disruptor.'"

Theron looked to Aigon, hoping that perhaps he would know what this meant, but his gaze was blank. It did not register.

"A disruptor," Theron repeated.

"You're trying to kill the Dark Captain, aren't you?" the farmer's wife said. "You're following him. Well, I wish you luck. May Amara speed you to victory…"

He would need more than this woman's blessings. But words couldn't hurt.

GREAT KORTHOS ROAD

Gaia's servants had openly laughed at her when she emerged from the inn's cellar, her shoes gone, her dress cut threadbare and her face marred with soot. They had even questioned her about the thing she was holding… the dreaded Gauntlet which the Demiurge wanted.

As she bumped along in the carriage, on her way back to the city, it struck her… how was she to deliver the Gauntlet to a creature which existed only in her dreams?

She took the Gauntlet from the bag she had stowed it in.

Even now, it was icy to the touch.

In terms of its crafting, the Gauntlet of the Demiurge was a masterwork. Divided into several plates, its black metal could guard a person's right hand while allowing maximum mobility. It was burnished and smooth, polished well—yet somehow it never sparkled in the sunlight. The blackness of the metal seemed to swallow all light.

She ran her hand along one of the Gauntlet's fingers—and it curled. Gaia screamed and dropped the Gauntlet on the floor. It had moved without her knowing… it had a mind of its own.

The carriage stopped. The curtain was pushed aside; and a servant entered.

"Are you all right, mistress?" he asked.

"Yes, fine!" Gaia snapped. "Now leave me alone… don't bother me again."

The servant shut the curtain and a few moments later, the carriage lurched into motion. The journey to Korthos would not last much longer, but it would all be spent in panic.

Would this Gauntlet strangle her in her sleep? Would the nightmares she had left behind be replaced with a greater one?

She grabbed the Gauntlet off the carriage floor and swiftly

tossed it back in its bag. She pulled the drawstring as tight as she could, but wondered if it would break out of its own accord and strangle her. Either way, it was clear she was not safe. This Gauntlet of the Demiurge, this artifact of an ancient age, was crafted by no human smith. A dark power had put his soul into it; and life had not yet left the Gauntlet.

A thread of spirit connected this Gauntlet to hell itself. Kronos—who according to the ancient poem, was bound in chains—still possessed power in the mortal world.

She cursed herself, never having thought of how she would give this Gauntlet to its owner: an entity who only appeared in nightmares, an entity who reached beyond hell, pointed to her, and sealed her to his own.

Kronos was the enemy of ancient heroes, the terror of Old Eloesus, the horror of the Archaic World. And now somehow, Kronos—the Demiurge—had impressed himself on Gaia. With a hand of black shadow he had pointed to her from beyond the material world, and infiltrated her psyche.

~

Back at home, having washed up and donned a fine crimson gown, and having ordered a servant to powder her face and braid her hair, Gaia stepped out onto the street.

The dangers of venturing out onto the streets alone, especially for a woman of high status, were considerable. But the Gauntlet was in her room, lying unrestrained atop her dresser. She needed protection, without the rumors of insanity which would certainly spread.

On Bellows Street, there was a smith who had forged horseshoes for her beasts of burden and knives for her kitchen servants.

When he received her request, at a cost of five *doukon*, he sold her just what she wanted: a lockbox of incredible strength and a key to go along with it, large enough to contain the Gauntlet. It was not ornamented with gold and silver, as she'd prefer, but she wasn't purchasing this for beauty—she was purchasing a lockbox to preserve her own life.

The smith did not ask the reason for her purchasing; he knew better. Yet Gaia had never made a similar purchase before.

~

The Gauntlet of the Demiurge had not moved from its place. It lay on the dresser, unmoved from its prior position.

Gaia wondered if she had merely imagined the finger curl up. Perhaps she was mad. But it was good to take precautions. Even if the Gauntlet's movement was mere delusion, she could not sleep with it nearby.

If the Gauntlet had a mind of its own, surely it could creep up on her in bed and wring her neck.

She set the lockbox on the dresser and, as quickly as she could, tossed the horrid Gauntlet of the Demiurge inside. With the key, she locked it tight, and made certain it wouldn't budge.

She could rest now. She could breathe.

She had retrieved the vile Gauntlet from the heart of Mount Kronos; but how could she deliver it to its master? Its master, the one who forged it, lived only in Gaia's dreams.

The sun had not set. Gaia had eaten only a bit of bread and a half a cup of wine. Yet the journey had taxed her to the limit.

Weary and sore, she undressed and donned her nightclothes. She shut the door to her bedroom, gave one wary look to the lockbox in front of her, and climbed in bed.

Within moments, she was asleep.

~

When she awoke, stomach quivering, paralyzed and weightless, horror came over her as she realized she had not escaped the demiurge's grip. She did not want to look at her bedroom door and watch the monster arrive, but her eyelids wouldn't shut.

A coldness crawled across the room in anticipation of the visitor.

When the shadow appeared, she screamed but no sound came out. Her mouth did not move; she was paralyzed and transfixed.

Gingerly the shadowy form stooped over her, its eyes burning red beacons, its breath as icy as death. Trembling, Gaia heard its long sigh, then its whisper… "Thou hast done as I asked."

Then release me! she wanted to scream, but her lips would not move, her throat could not make a noise.

"Thou dost not know the power of that which thou hast taken… power unthinkable to man. And now my Gauntlet, which thou has brought from my lair, thou must now use it…"

The restraint on her voice disappeared. She sucked in a deep breath. "You lied!" she cried. "You lied!"

"I am not yet in this world.

"Thou must put on my Gauntlet. Thou must wear it as armor on your hand."

"Never!" she screamed.

"Then thou must put it on another. It shall terrify him and destroy him, yet make him powerful.

"To him whom thou hatest above all, to him whom thou despiseth, to him whom thou loathe above all things… give the

Gauntlet to him. For the power shall come at a cost… he shall be utterly destroyed."

To him whom thou hatest. The demiurge's words conjured up one name and one face alone… Rogon.

Rogon, who had betrayed her. Rogon, who had spurned her openly. Rogon, who had driven her into public disgrace.

"I hate Rogon," she said. "I hate Rogon more than anyone in this world…"

"Then give it unto him," said the demiurge. "Give it to him; and he shall have power. Yet despite this power, he shall be destroyed."

The nightmare slipped away. Her fear left her. She drifted into a deep sleep.

~

Shafts of morning light were peeking through the curtains, revealing a blue sky.

The sound of banging metal had awoken her.

In her revulsion she saw that the lockbox was quivering.

The Gauntlet of the Demiurge—having achieved some semblance of life—was trying its best to escape.

Who knew if the lockbox could hold? A power animated the Gauntlet, a power greater than Gaia or any mortal. How could a lockbox prevent its escape? How could a lockbox, made by human hands, halt the work of the demiurge?

The dread had banished her morning exhaustion. Alert and energized, Gaia hopped out of her bed. She grabbed the key and opened the lockbox. She would deliver the Gauntlet of the Demiurge to Rogon.

Power, it would give him… and then he would be destroyed.

HIGH CITY, THÉNAI

As a young woman, in Tigris, no one had considered Khloë a great beauty. Though she had no trouble attracting men, she had been considered plain.

Now, Kunar, King of the Thenoans, had taken a liking to her. Outside the House of the Archon—now "the palace"—she had taken a brief respite from the incessant party.

The air was chilly and the wind forceful this high up. Khloë was not dressed well for the weather.

Kunar had found her exotic looks enticing. Dark-haired and swarthy, she looked unlike any Eloesian woman. The thin brassiere and loin she wore exposed her muscular arms and belly. In human women, such figure would appear abominable; but in an amazon warrior, King Kunar's court found it attractive.

How repulsive was Kunar… obese, aging, with a red beard. He had not yet forced himself upon her. What would she do if her artful escapes and excuses wore thin? She had not even lain with Theron—a man she revered, maybe even loved. The thought of Kunar's fingers touching her skin, the idea of anything approximating close contact, made her want to wretch.

This situation—from captive to prize—had all started when Kunar apprehended her.

"Where is Theron?" his torturers had asked repeatedly.

And when they became convinced she didn't know, Kunar had taken a liking to her.

The thought of him sickened her.

"Khloë!" shouted someone from inside the palace. "Khloë! Come in!"

~

Kunar was drunk.

A jar of wine was in one hand; with the other he was flinging pottery at a target set up several yards away. He was hunched over, shirtless, revealing his enormous belly.

Top officials were in the room with him: the Politarch of Food and Wine, currying favor with king through these undignified antics; a prominent demiarch, dancing and playing a lyre horribly; even a Stratego in charge of a large battalion, guzzling from a jar of wine and prancing stupidly in the center of the room.

On a rack, the Stratego's fur coat was hanging from a peg. Khloë seized it and wrapped it around her shoulders. Despite massive fire burning in the hearth, the wintry chill was omnipresent.

Here, Khloë was vulnerable and alone.

If monstrous Kunar forced himself on her, she could easily kill him. But the regicide would provoke the Eloesian army to slay her on the spot.

She would not drink wine, either, for fear that her guard would be let down.

And so she stood here, in her private prison, hoping against hope that Theron was alive.

She feared more than anything that Kunar would seize upon her… that he would force himself upon her. What choice would she have but to go along? The thought of that scratchy red beard, that hairy belly, that white corpselike skin sent a chill through her body, a chill colder than the wintry air.

To her horror, she saw that Kunar was gazing at her. "Come closer, my sweet!"

What could she do?

There were hoplites at the exit; there were hoplites posted at each corner of the room. Kunar's most loyal bodyguard would never see harm come to him; or would they?

Many in Thénai thought Kunar's so-called "kingship" was illegitimate. But none would ever admit that publicly.

She braced herself and approached Kunar. He took a swig of wine from the jar, emptying all its contents until a red trickle streamed from his beard. He belched and then hurled the wine jar at the makeshift target, missing badly. It shattered in a hundred pieces on the floor.

Kunar swung around to face Khloë.

What made this man so revolting was that he called himself a king; yet he put all responsibility in the hands of his deputies.

Kunar leaned in to kiss her but Khloë jerked away.

She questioned whether she should have allowed it; but Kunar quickly shut his eyes and collapsed. He had drunk too much wine. Though it was still only afternoon, he wouldn't wake up until the next morning. His daily drinking parties were seeming to exhaust him earlier and earlier; it was all for Khloë's good. But seeing him in his stupor made him all the more repulsive.

In Amazonia, heavy drinking was considered a stain on your character—next to cowardice, it was worthy of social ostracism. Even though Eloesians considered it a point of pride to drink others under the table, the constant parties of Kunar were seen as distasteful.

Khloë could not see the faces behind the helmets, but she wondered if the bodyguards had ever considered a coup.

This oaf surely didn't add anything to the success of Thénai and the Thenoan League. What was the point in keeping him alive?

The hoplites did not move; they were silent and perfectly still, like statues.

They would not harm the one they'd been sworn to protect.

But a seed had been planted in Khloë's heart; and that seed would grow.

The Thenoan League, the city itself, and the world, would be better without Kunar.

A dagger in the heart… or poison in his cup.

No. She could not. She didn't have the courage.
Or did she?

THE GOLDEN ROAD, OUTSIDE THENAI

Having left the hill country behind, Rogon and his six-thousand soldiers had drawn near the coast. The air had acquired a salt smell and a cooling wind was blowing from the west, even as signs of spring had appeared.

As trees blossomed and the grass had turned a bright shade of green, as flowers bloomed in the fields and bees buzzed around their hives, an impending sense of doom was all around them. War was coming. Rogon was certain of his victory; but it would come at a terrible cost. How many of his men, how many hoplites, would fall during the Siege of Thénai?

The farms around him were empty; no one was sowing spring crops. All had withdrawn, fleeing in a panic to whatever walled towns would take them; caught by surprise, the Thenoans had retreated to fortresses and hidden keeps.'

Rogon's guides said the city lay some five miles away. If they moved fast and marched all day, they could reach the walls by sundown.

It was the fifth of Alphaios. The New Year had come and gone. No doubt the arrival of Rogon's army had banished the celebration of their heathen feast.

And all those weeks and months ago, a date had been set that—Athra will it—when Rogon arrived unscathed in enemy territory, the Kersican Navy would attack and blockade. That date had been set for the thirteenth of Alphaios. Everything had fallen into place; but Rogon had arrived a week before planned. Like all his endeavors, he had succeeded beyond his expectations; through a forced march, he had crossed the mountain road in less time than any expected.

It was time to make an example.

Thénai was surrounded by farms; this had to change. Unopposed and unchallenged, Rogon had free reign over the land.

"Burn everything down!" Rogon shouted, turning to the column of hoplites behind him.

They did not hesitate. Instantly, the orderly column which had stretched far into the distance dispersed into a hundred different paths.

Within the hour, they all brandished torches and flaming sticks.

By sundown—after much effort—everything began to burn. And burn. And burn.

The farmhouses caught on fire. The crops had burned to dust. The silos and barns had turned to towers of flame.

In the night sky, under a cloak of stars, everything was burning. Everything was on fire. Everything had turned to flame.

HIGH CITY, THÉNAI

In times of crisis, when all seems lost, true character is revealed.

Kunar had left in the night. No one knew where he had gone.

Faced with the possibility of a city under siege, he had fled. A city depending on him was left scrambling for answers.

And Khloë—still wearing the brassiere and loin that the fat coward had dressed him in—watched as certain doom approached.

Far in the distance, fires had started, fires so intense and widespread they were visible from Khloë's vantage point. The Dark Captain, the Butcher of Nissos, was laying waste to all of Thénai's farmland, all the sources of its food and wealth. He would not rest until the city was razed to the ground.

He would butcher Thénai like he'd butchered Nissos. With Kunar gone, with defenses failing, with morale on the verge of collapse, they would fall before the Dark Captain; the fire would spread to the city gates, and then devour them whole.

FIVE MILES FROM THÉNAI

Following the Dark Captain all this way with Aigon by his side, Theron became convinced of two things.

Rogon was obsessed with fire; he revered it like a god.

That explained the burning inferno which lit up the night and—for a short while—made Theron doubt his cover. He had withdrawn into the bushes, though still the brightness of the burning fields made everything as light as day. The light threatened to uncover him and reveal his location; but Theron wouldn't run.

The form of the Dark Captain with his mantis-like helmet was an outline against the flame.

He stared at his work worshipfully even as his men scurried this way and that.

His reverence for fire had become clear.

Also clear: the Oracle's servants had his ear.

The Maids of the Mount of Prophecy had visited his camp twice since Theron began tracking them.

Somehow, the threat of the Oracle and the threat of Rogon and his vile Korthians had become intertwined.

Aigon had cautioned at all times against bringing harm to the Maids of Prophecy.

Theron had listened. He knew as well as Aigon of the great power which the Oracle possessed. He could not betray his location or his intent. A murdered Maid of Prophecy would do just that. The trail of blood would lead directly to Theron and his intentions; and his intentions would lead directly to him.

Silently he watched shadow of the Dark Captain, an inky silhouette against the flame. From this vantage point, Rogon appeared like a giant bug. The antennae of his helmet, his bulky greaves and gauntlets, even the giant sword clipped to his side, caused him to resemble an insect. No doubt it was intentional, an act to inspire terror in his enemies.

But the raging inferno he had created would surely fill Thénai with much greater dread.

Aigon tapped Theron on the shoulder. "We should leave. We may be compromised."

But this time, Theron would not listen. He was not Aigon's slave; he was not Aigon's ward.

He watched as Rogon's hoplites fled from the searing heat they had created, while Rogon stood firm, brave and invulnerable to the flame. The fire did not bother him. He seemed untouchable. His creation, which was devastating Thénai, was surely burning his skin; yet he remained still and unfazed. Fire, his god, would bring no harm to him.

Aigon had an arrow already nocked to his bow. Somehow, he thought Theron was going to get them in trouble.

Theron wondered if he was strong enough to slay Rogon when he had all these helping hands. So many thousands of hoplites with shields and spears, and surely Theron—whom Aigon called a hero—would fall.

As the hoplites dispersed, driven away like flies before a torch, Theron watched as Rogon became increasingly alone. The heat and flame had driven them from their master. They began retreating to the hills, far from sight.

Aigon's cautioning hand restrained Theron. Aigon knew what his ward wanted to do.

The hoplites had retreated to the camp. Theron had this one opportunity. Alone and vulnerable, the Dark Captain was prime prey for Theron's club.

Pushing past Aigon's restraint, Theron lurched forward. Open and un-hidden in the grass, he drew closer and closer to

Rogon. The heat grew in intensity, until it had become a physical force.

Soon, Theron was within just yards of Rogon. If he had a stone to throw, he could slay Rogon right here. But the ground around him was dry grass, with only pebbles to offer.

And the heat—already searing—would likely burn Theron to death if he drew any closer.

Or so it seemed. He could endure incredible heat; he had entered the caldera of Mount Kronos and stood just fathoms above the liquid fire. A well placed blow of the club, shattering the helmet, could crush Rogon and splinter his army. The attack on Thénai could end… and finally, months after the Battle of Maratha, Theron could claim his revenge.

But though the Dark Captain was an enemy of Eloesus, Theron didn't take another step.

It wasn't honorable to kill an enemy on unequal footing. A true man of bravery would meet him head on, in battle.

Rogon raised his hands. He was praying in the Fharese language. But who was he praying to? What god loved destruction and death?

Theron turned around, intending to back away, when he sensed something changed.

He turned back and saw Rogon facing him. In the bright flame, which would burn to death any normal man, he appeared like a shadow, the silhouette of a great bug. With one stroke he drew his greatsword. Were things coming to a head?

Had the time of battle arrived? They were both equally prepared. The stronger man would win.

"Not now," said Rogon. "Not yet."

Theron agreed. He nodded his head and turned.

Aigon joined Theron as they walked into the outlying hills.

Their battle would come another day.

HIGH CITY, THÉNAI

The burning of the fields had faded, turning the landscape beyond Thénai's walls to smoldering ash. Khloë, from her high vantage point, felt pensive.

It had been thirteen days since the New Year's celebration. It was then that the first reports of the Dark Captain arrived… that he had somehow crossed the treacherous mountain passes and emerged with a sizeable army, strong enough to threaten the world.

It was then that Kunar had proven himself a coward. At the first sight of danger, the heavy-drinking, loud-mouthed Kunar had become silent and pallid, fearful of his shadow, afraid of every loud noise. Now he was gone; having abdicated all his responsibilities, he had left the defense of the city to his Strategoi and hoplites.

He had proven himself a craven coward; he was a slug and not a man. Over the days and weeks that Khloë had been his fixation, she had grown to detest him.

Now, from Khloë's high perch on the roof of the world, she could see the vast, smoldering ruins of fields which surrounded the city along the coastal plain. Amid the ash and burnt blackness, columns of hoplites were approaching, and with them, wheeled engines, catapults and siege towers pulled by oxen.

The Thenoan League's brave Strategoi had taken the place of leadership that Kunar had abdicated.

All along the circuit wall, archers were posted on the battlements.

The women and children of the city had taken shelter in doors; all those fathoms beneath Khloë's feet, no one was stirring. The busy, packed streets and rife commerce were gone.

It struck Khloë, after all this time, that she had no supervision.

Kunar's bodyguard had left with him. Only hoplites guarding the temple watched over her.

Khloë's sabers were somewhere inside the House of the Archon. She had seen a passing glimpse of them one day, early in her captivity. One of Kunar's servants had stowed them away. No doubt Kunar, ever the coward, was afraid she'd get her hands on them and escape. Kunar could never overpower her, nor could his bodyguards man-for-man.

The afternoon light was casting shadows against the Temple of Tyros and the House of the Archon. The sun's journey across the heavens was nearing completion. The warmth of the spring day was fading away. As darkness began to set in, cloaking the world in mystery, Khloë took her chance; she slipped away through the door, into the House of the Archon. She would find her sabers. She would return, armed. She would battle for Thénai. She would battle for the distant hope that Theron might return.

~

The candles had all burnt out, and what little light entered the House of the Archon was that of the dim afternoon sun, filtering through windows.

She could still hear voices of servants in the halls, and the clatter of pots and pans, but compared to just yesterday, things were eerily quiet. In the distance, through the vast network of corridors, shadows darted to and fro; but the place seemed empty in comparison. The government officials had left. The Strategoi and politarchs who frequented Kunar's drinking parties had all gone away, for the sake of defending the city. A pall of dread had fallen over the entire city; but none more, it seemed, than the House of the Archon.

In the foyer, a nearly burnt-out candle offered a dim light.

Hurriedly, Khloë ran up and grabbed it, blowing on it to revive the flame. This would be her sole illumination.

The armor which she had brought from Amazonia—crafted from leather and iron plates—was gone. Kunar's men had likely sold it in the market; but the sabers, perhaps because of their exceptional quality, they had kept for themselves.

Over the weeks she had spent in the House of the Archon, she'd become accustomed to the comings and goings. As the center of the Thenoan League, it possessed many secrets. Though designed like a humble house to banish all appearances of monarchy, it was so much more, and beneath Khloë's feet there were chambers, rooms and labyrinths. She had overheard Kunar, one late night, speaking of a prison which—somehow—existed beneath the floors of the House.

One night, while—in her quest for distraction—she had begun to clean the hallways, she knocked over a painting and discovered, behind a panel, a secret passageway. For a moment, she'd entertained the idea of climbing in and finding out where it led. That sounded crazy, then… but not so much now.

She walked around the House of the Archon for an hour. In each room, she scoured cupboards and cabinets for any sign of the sabers. She came up empty. Even in rooms where she'd been forbidden, now un-guarded, she'd found no trace of them.

So, if the sabers weren't in the House of the Archon, and they hadn't sold them to the market, they had to be somewhere in the labyrinth below. Or so Khloë guessed.

It was a wild guess, she admitted. A guess which was more than likely wrong. But still, in the shadows of the night, she found herself walking through the halls with a renewed purpose. In a corner of the room, she found the painting.

In terms of artistry, it was beautiful: framed in gold, it depicted the goddess Amara in the ancient Garden of the Gods when the deities supposedly walked the earth. She was depicted as a battle maiden, in full armor, with a spear and shield. The colors, even in the dim light of the sconces, were bright and luminous. Her bronze helm was as green as leaves on a tree; her blue eyes as bright as the sky. In the Garden of the Gods, there were no evils for her to vanquish, no enemies to subdue. Yet the artist had brought her to vivid life.

And, in exchange for his genius, the Thenoans had used his work as a foil.

Gently, Khloë removed the painting from the wall. The secret passageway was revealed, a tight-fitting space which faded into inky blackness. Where would it lead? Where would it take her? Goddess only knew.

~

Through the blackness she crawled, squirming through the narrow, airless chamber. Two times she stopped in exhaustion, fearing she'd suffocate. The passageway had taken many twists and turns and finally had begun to descend: down, down, down she crawled, and it seemed her journey would never end.

Sweating and unable to breathe, even the brassiere and loin she wore seemed restrictive.

She began to wonder if the passageway was a death trap, designed to kill the curious; then light appeared—dim flames, a cavernous ceiling, a pool.

Torches were lighting up this subterranean chamber, carved out of the High City's rock. The smoke from the flame was filtered through a shaft in the vast ceiling above. A makeshift palace with columns and tiered floors towered over the pool; and there, swimming and splashing, was Kunar. His bodyguards stood still and silent; in the dim light they were only shadowy silhouettes. On either side of the miniature palace, there were wooden casks piled on top of wooden casks—no doubt holding wine, Kunar's one true passion, the only thing he cared about.

Here, in this secret chamber which he had no doubt carved out for himself on the backs of slaves, he could avoid his responsibility; he could preserve his life, even while his city teetered on the brink.

"There she is!" The repulsive slug was waving at her.

She had no choice now but to enter Kunar's private chamber, this hollowed-out hole where he escaped the responsibilities that had been thrust upon him.

A staircase had been chiseled out of rock; by a twisting, turning route, Khloë descended to the ground floor of the chamber.

Though she did not want to, Khloë crossed the distance between them, over the carved-tile floor and finally, up to the edge of the pool.

"You've found my secret home." Kunar was smirking.

Through a window of the miniature palace, she made out the face of one of Kunar's favorite courtesans, a dark-haired devotee of the pleasure goddess Isdar. Through other windows, up above, there were more girls that he favored.

Wine and women, he had stowed away in his lair. Those were the things he loved best.

"And to think," said Kunar, "I got this done during my tenure as king. Fifty slaves brought in from Korthos, working all day and all night. It only took them five months."

Khloë could no longer hide her disgust. "The people of Thénai are terrified…"

"They are in good hands."

"They should be in *your* hands."

Rather than angered, Kunar appeared amused. He chuckled lightly. It seemed the apparent safety of the hideaway had taken away his fear. "Come," Kunar said, his head bobbing in the water, his arms splashing, "join me."

A wave of revulsion passed through her. "No," she answered.

Kunar's amusement vanished. "Don't forget that I'm king."

Khloë sneered. "Your Majesty. I came into captivity with two priceless objects. Two sabers, carved with foreign letters. Sabers which cannot be bought anywhere else. Sabers which could slice that beard from your face in one cut. And they are gone."

Kunar stepped out of the pool toward her. His belly sagged, covering almost half of his legs. White and hairy, he was monstrous to behold in his nudity. The Thenoans sculpted pictures of handsome, athletic youths; Kunar, their king, was the exact opposite.

Khloë found herself backing away. She recognized the lust in his eyes.

"Go away," Khloë muttered. "Stay back."

Kunar knew he could never overpower her; but as king, his loyal bodyguards were always there to step in. He knew this. He saw her pain; he enjoyed it. He didn't think she'd have the nerve to fight back.

She questioned the wisdom of doing so, as he lurched forward step by step. Words could not stop him. There was no convincing. He was accustomed to taking what he wanted. She wondered, for a moment, whether it would be best to go along with this, to save her life, to reserve her place in Thénai. But as soon as one of his fat fingers touched her skin, she knew beyond doubt that whatever dangers it posed, she could not let him step an inch closer.

As a girl, trained to be a warrior, she had been taught to

fight not just with swords and spears but also with her bare hands. She could kill with a punch.

And yet a sword was clipped to Kunar's side; an Eloesian broadsword. The hilt was in reach.

She rushed him, nearly knocking him over, and drew the sword from its sheath.

In her hands, the weapon was awkward. Off balance and unsure in her grip, the weapon was foreign to her. But quickly she gained control. She swung back the blade. She imagined his head separated from its body.

She caught sight of a door to the far right of the cavern. She dropped the sword and ran.

She would not kill him. Some strange part of her would not allow it.

Through the door Khloë bolted, down further passageways, until at last, an hour later, she found herself in a cave amid the hills outside the city. The crickets were chirping and the air smelled of sweet pollen. The stars were bright amid the dark expanse of the sky. The moon was bright and full. In the wilderness, there was peace. Even as the Korthian soldiers encamped around Thénai, even as flames and smoke could be seen in the harbor, Khloë was nothing if not tranquil.

She had become a citizen of two cities; she had lost them both. It was time to go home to Amazonia.

CITY WALL, THÉNAI

In a trance, as Rogon watched his work, seeing the burning fields, he had been enveloped in the moment. As the fire encapsulated the world around him, as the heat became searing in his intensity, he had been enraptured by this act of worship to the Nameless God.

In that moment, it appeared he had hallucinated. He had a vision of Theron—his mortal enemy—challenging him to combat, man for man. His ancient nemesis had been wearing a lion's skin on his head and nothing more than a loin cloth covering his body. In his hand, he had held a fearsome club.

Where had he envisioned this? Where had he come up with the image of Theron, wearing a lion's skin?

It did not matter. If it was a message from the Nameless God, it surely was designed to confuse.

He and his men had encamped along the city. Defenders on the walls, far above, waited and watched with bows in hand.

Last night, ships had arrived and decimated the Thenoan Navy; using a fire that burned in water, which Rogon had explained how to create, they had destroyed everything wooden and flammable for a mile. The poor Korthian sailors had no idea what it would do to them.

Other sailors, in the know, arrived later and prevented any ships from going or leaving. The city was surrounded; and soon it would starve.

The walls stretched to a towering height above Rogon. The short winter had passed and the sun had grown in its intensity. Soon, and very soon, they would offer their terms of surrender. They would beg for mercy and they would receive none.

All along the walls, near the white-stone parapets, faces had been carved—some sticking out their tongues, others glaring or leering. A crow was perched on one of those stone tongues, its marble-like eyes watching over Rogon's men. The superstitious would say it was a bad sign, an omen of impending disaster. But Rogon did not read omens. He did not give them credence.

Once, before he exterminated the male population of Sharam-El and sold the survivors into slavery, he had believed in omens. A holy man had strewn grain across the dry desert ground and set a chicken before it. "If the chicken eats the grain, we will succeed," the holy man had said. "If she refuses, we will fail."

When the chicken refused, Rogon—in his anger—had slain the chicken and thrown it into the sea. Ignoring the advice, he had besieged Sharam-El... and succeeded despite everyone's suggestions. It was his first victory and one that brought him into high favor before the King of Kings.

Yet as the crow shifted its feet and then took off, flying toward the foothills, a shiver passed down Rogon's spine.

Up on the battlements, the defenders on the walls had begun stamping their feet. They were singing together, in true Eloesian fashion. Rogon could not understand the ancient dialect they used, but predictably he heard the words "Phillipidēs!" and "Amara" and "imperishable fame." The Eloesians—even the ones he fought with—were preoccupied with stories and fables. They spent their wealth not on vast armies but on statues and vast concert halls.

Their victory in the Southron War was pure luck. When all the strength of the King of Kings was meted out and delivered on the battlefield, Eloesus would fail; and it too would become part of the Southern World.

Rogon looked up again at the top of the wall, seeing the Thenoan archers standing nervously at the ready. They knew their doom was near. Rogon would deliver it to them.

FOOTHILLS OF MOUNT BARKALOS, THENOA

From his perch in the shade of a holm oak, Theron watched a black bird fly in from the south and land on Aigon's arm.

The centaur was whispering to the crow, speaking in hushed whispers, in a language unintelligible to human ears.

Far in the distance, beneath their feet, on the edge of the sprawling coastal plain, Thénai was a city besieged. Though the harbor was burning, and an army had amassed around its walls, Thénai was far from Theron, in distance and in mind.

Did it matter whether Thénai burned? If the temple was robbed of its gold, if its marble monuments were reduced to pebbles, did it affect Theron at all?

Yet something had brought him here. Something had caused him to travel all this way.

Once he had been a citizen of Thénai. Now... what was he? What was he, besides Aigon's ward?

The crow on Aigon's hand was murmuring in the way that only crows could. Aigon's pointed ears were pushed back as he listened to every sound.

On the road with Aigon, many birds had landed on his arm. Does and fawns had approached without a modicum of fear, only hesitating if they saw Theron. Beavers left their lodges and ran up to Aigon, chattering in their own language. Their love and trust of the centaur had overwhelmed their natural fear of man.

And moreover, though Aigon never explicitly told him, Theron suspected that the conversations he had with these animals went both ways. Somehow, he knew the language that philosophers had striven to understand: the tongue of beasts.

And if he did understand the crow's cooing, it was natural

to him. Centaurs resembled mankind, at least in part; but they were very different. They were ancient; and they gave no credence or honor to gods and goddesses. Aigon, the last of the centaurs, had never said a word about Amara or Nix. He spoke reverently only of Phillipidēs—in his words, "His greatest failure" in that he failed to protect him.

The crow flew away, north toward the snow-capped mountains.

Aigon turned toward Theron. His hooves kicked up dust in the dry ground.

"There is someone following us."

No doubt the crow had told him that. Somehow, through those coos and warblings, a message had reached Aigon's ears.

Theron was sick of fleeing whenever danger approached. "Let her come." If the Maid of Prophecy wanted trouble, she'd find it.

GATE OF STORMS, KORTHOS

Without fanfare or commotion, Gaia's coach left its familiar moorings in the city she called home, and set out for the impossibly long trip to Thénai.

Thénai, Korthos' ancient rival, was indeed her destination.

In front of her, hidden under a blanket in the carriage car, the lockbox which contained the Gauntlet of the Demiurge rattled and shook on the floor.

Her terror had passed. The Gauntlet would not break free, as much as it tried.

She would deliver it to her greatest enemy. She would ensure that it destroyed him.

POWER

The student had pleased his teacher. He had uncovered the meaning of truth and falsehood. Perhaps, he could finally acquire his diploma, after all these years of study and hard work.

"Is it time? Have I finally done everything you asked?" asked the student underneath the olive tree.

"You have discovered what truth and falsehood is," said the philosopher. "Now what is knowledge?"

"Knowledge?" said the student. "Knowledge is power."

Later that day he received his diploma, a roll of rawhide. He had finally accomplished what he'd sought after, years after he'd begun.

SUN KING'S ROAD, KORTHICA

As the carriage rattled along the road, Gaia took frequent looks outside the shuttered windows.

The road on in Korthica was paved with white stones, some parts more fastidiously than others. Once they reached Kersica, it was a different story. Preferring practicality to beauty, the Kersicans left it in dirt.

Funerary monuments, crypts, and mausoleums were built along the roadside to her left and right. No one knew exactly how and why this custom had begun. Each man or woman of wealth intended to stun passersby with the grandeur of their resting place; but what was the point, now that they were dust, eaten by worms?

There were mysteries on this road, this road she'd traveled many times before. Its name was a mystery in itself. The Sun King's Road? Who was the Sun King? Many stories had been told, many fables written to explain. But few facts were out there and noting was for certain. All reasoning put forth was pure speculation.

Six days after the journey began, they crossed the border into Kersica.

Just years ago, such a venture would be dangerous; any unaccompanied person ran the risk of being captured and sold into slavery as an Elehoi.

Now, having forged an unlikely alliance against the unlikely rising power of Thénai, it was safe. Gaia, a valued member of that alliance, would have no hair on her head harmed.

That night, they camped on the open road, amid the green hills. Hoplites were posted all around Gaia and her servants, keeping watch for bandits.

After a meal cooked over an open fire and a glass of watered-down wine, Gaia had returned to her carriage and folded out her bed. Her servants were sleeping outside in blankets when there was a knock on the carriage door.

When she opened it, her servant Pagos was standing there. The young man had a look of worry on his face. "My mistress…"

For some reason, Gaia was moved. "Come in," she said.

"I'm afraid," he began.

Gaia expected fear of bandits; but for a servant to express it, and a man no less…

The lockbox began jolting and shaking.

The servant backed away in panic.

That, Gaia realized, is what he feared.

"What is that?" said Pagos. "I've never seen anything like it before… What's in it? Is it an animal?"

But the sound of metal ringing against metal made it clear, it was something else entirely.

"Everyone is afraid," Pagos ventured to say. "Can you tell me what's in it? Or toss it aside…"

Gaia sighed. "Don't worry," she said. "It's tucked away in the lockbox. It can't hurt you."

"What is it?" Pagos repeated.

But Gaia couldn't tell him. If she told him, the panic would spread. What lie could she come up with? "It's a mechanism… an invention," she said off the spur of the moment. "It was created by the great inventor Agenor…" Surely he'd believe the man who created the colossus and the City Crusher could invent something like this.

But Pagos was looking at her skeptically. Quietly, he

withdrew and shut the carriage door.

As Gaia donned her nightclothes and prepared to sleep, the lockbox jerking to and fro unnerved her far more than she wanted to admit; and after she finally drifted off hours later, her dreams were dark and troubled.

CITY WALL, THÉNAI

The sun was beating down harshly outside Thénai's towering walls.

Rogon and his men had sat encamped around the city for two weeks now. Their idleness had begun to wear on them. They had joined the army for the thrill of battle; now—according to Rogon's wishes—they wouldn't storm the city but instead starve it out until they accepted terms of surrender.

In a city with so many people, they would give up hope sooner than not.

That did not stop his men from becoming restless.

~

It was late in that spring day when horns blew across the city walls, from every turret.

Out of nowhere, it seemed—or a postern gate—a group of horsemen came riding toward Rogon. In their hands they bore flags of Thénai, flapping in the wind: a gold laurel wreath set against a blue background.

Some hoplites were grabbing javelins.

"Stop!" Rogon shouted. Allowing your enemy to speak was the first rule of honorable combat.

Flanked by horsemen, the king of Thénai was riding ahead.

Rogon had never met King Kunar nor seen him. He was as unimpressive as the rumors stated. He looked far too big for the horse he was riding. His only remarkable feature was the jeweled crown he wore.

The Thenoans and most Eloesians had always hated any signs of royalty or kingship. It seemed, with Kunar, that had all changed.

He struck a sad figure, his body lurching over the saddle, clearly struggling to stay on. He made a pathetic ambassador for the Thenoan people. It was better that way; Rogon could speak from a position of strength.

When they arrived, it took three men to help Kunar off his horse. He staggered and stumbled at first, then waddled over to Rogon. An ill-fitting sword was clipped to his belt in a sheath; a chainmail shirt stretched tightly across his belly. He was trying to give the impression of a warrior but failing badly. Standing there in the heat, facing Rogon, he was panting and clearly exhausted. But it had taken a small bit of bravery to come here at all.

"Rogon," said Kunar, "I have come to offer my terms…"

Rogon smiled. "Of course," he said.

An hour of supplications, begging and deferment, and they had outlined their terms.

"You will live on as king," Rogon repeated, "but under the sovereign control of the Kersican League."

Within days, Kunar would open the gates; he would betray his people. This was pleasing to Rogon; but it also proved the softness of Eloesians, the cowardice and selfishness.

"A nation of actors and pederasts is destined to fall," his master, the King of Kings, once said.

And it was true. In the face of true difficulty, they would buckle and break. Kunar would deliver his city to the Kersican League, and then Rogon would deliver the nation to the southrons.

ARAPIS PLAIN

As a child, Theron had heard stories of the Arapis Plain; how, when the gods formed the earth, a tear fell from Alabastros' eye and gave life and rich soil to an area where there had been none before.

Vineyards and wheat fields filled this rich land, in the shadow of Mount Tharnos' snow-capped peak. Spring planting had begun, despite the war and bloodshed just miles away.

And Theron was running away, though he did not want to. He was fleeing the one who doggedly pursued him: a woman, Aigon said, sent from the Mount of Prophecy.

On the Arapis Plain, there were plenty of places to slip away. There were walled villages throughout the plain, and a network of roads and paths. Eventually, they would lose her.

Aigon had convinced him to flee; it was not an easy choice. Theron could easily defeat her; but the Mount of Prophecy would uncover his trail. Or so he reasoned.

Late in the day, as they passed a walled village, a pair of eagles came flying up to Aigon, then landed gently on his arm. They began to screech, and Aigon's ears perked forward to listen.

Aigon spoke to them in that whispering language that seemed to roll off his tongue.

In time they flew away. It seemed all the earth's creatures were Aigon's friends and dedicated servants.

Aigon trotted around to face Theron. He looked confused. "I was wrong," he said.

He didn't often admit that.

At dusk, their pursuer appeared.

The form of an amazon was clear, with a chakram in her

left hand and a dagger in the other. Theron's heart sank and his eyes watered as the form of Khloë appeared in the moonlight.

He dropped his club and ran up to her in a weeping embrace.

Khloë was weeping too. "It's been so long," she said through sobs. "I thought you were dead."

Theron pulled back and looked into her watering eyes; though dark they held a warm gleam. "Your swords are gone…"

"My greatest loss," said Khloë, "except you."

~

Khloë could hardly believe it. When she found the tuft of lion's hair, a little hope had been kindled in her heart. But despite all these days of tracking them, she never thought the time would come. Here he was; here she was. They were together.

Only after they had wept and embraced for a while did she see the creature accompanying him.

She had seen something like this creature in pictures and statues. For a second, too stunned to move or speak, she gawked at the creature which towered above Theron: its body like that of a horse, from the torso up like a human man. Could this truly be a centaur? Neither Khloë nor her amazon sisters, nor the Eloesians on the mainland, had considered centaurs anything more than legend.

Yet one was standing before her, a bow in his hand, a quiver strapped to his back, his ears pointed, his complexion dark and swarthy. His eyes, despite his dark features, were a bright piercing blue. His sandy-brown hair was roughly-shorn and stood up on end. There was a presence about him, a presence Khloë could not describe. His aura was powerful. A great creature stood before her… one who deserved reverence.

Though there wasn't a wrinkle on his face, Khloë could tell he was old. Ancient, even.

"Khloë," Theron said, "this is Aigon."

Khloë dropped to one knee; why, she didn't know. She had heard that name before; and somewhere, in some painting or bronze statue, she had seen him.

Aigon regarded her with a look of confusion. Perhaps centaurs had other ways of showing respect. He clopped over to her, and in his shadow she realized how huge he was. No warrior could defeat a creature like this, not even Theron.

"An Eloesian and an amazon, friends… That's a sight I've never seen." His voice was deep and commanding.

Khloë stood up and backed away from his mighty shadow. "We fought once, to the death," Khloë said. "Now, we are allies… at least, some of us are."

It was true the alliance—if there was one—continued only tenuously. So many humans harbored old hatreds, despising amazons and calling for war as if it were still archaic times. How many glares, how many dark looks had she witnessed on the streets of Korthos and Thénai? On the mainland, humans viewed amazons as threatening barbarians; in Amazonia, humans were viewed as filth.

"Many years can end ancient hatreds," said Aigon, but somehow he sounded unconvinced.

Perhaps the centaurs were old enough to remember the wars between amazons and humans, when Khloë's people were driven from the mainland by settlers and forced into hiding. For her people it was a bitter memory, still, all these decades and centuries later.

"What's happened to Thénai?" asked Theron.

~

The words, when they came from his lips, surprised him. Hadn't he left that old life behind? Hadn't he declared, on numerous occasions, that the nation was dead to him, that he hated Eloesus and its laurel wreath flag? Hadn't he told Aigon he hoped Thénai and Korthos both went up in smoke?

But he had asked. And he knew why. He could not forget the image of that demagogue, standing on a podium and railing against Thénai's enemies. Kunar was his name… for some reason, his crazed voice, his red beard, was imprinted in Theron's mind.

"It's still standing," Khloë said, "or it was."

Her voice was uncertain.

"But it has fallen," Theron ventured to guess, "in some way."

"Kunar."

"He has changed things," Khloë said. She eyed the ground pensively. "The people are in despair. They were, even before the Dark Captain arrived. Kunar's bled everyone dry to enrich himself. The people have grown hungry."

The image of Kunar standing before the lectern, clenched fist raised and shaking at the heavens, his face blood-red from anger, returned to Theron's mind. There was something about that image, something about that man, which was of great consequence.

An eagle was flying to the southwest, toward the coast.

The gleaming sea was calling him home.

He could not leave Thénai completely behind. Hero or not, he was still a Thenoan. His heart was still etched with the blue and gold of the Eloesian flag.

"We have to stop him," Theron said.

"I think I know a way," Khloë answered.

CITY WALL, THÉNAI

To Rogon's impatient men, who craved bloodshed, it seemed the siege had reached a standstill. The archers were posted all along the wall, arrows nocked to their bows, and seemed fully energized, with good morale; but behind the vestige of protection and safety, everything was crumbling.

Soon, within days, Kunar would have his closest confidantes open the gates; the Thenoan army would be crushed, and Rogon would assume control of the Thenoan League, with Kunar as his puppet.

Around noon, as the sun's heat built in intensity, there was a trumpet peal, crisp and clear. He recognized its timbre.

His men did too.

They did not halt the woman, riding in on a white horse, dressed head to toe in a blue gown. Her head and hair was bound up in an azure scarf, and the trumpet in her left hand was of sparkling silver. This young maid had been here before; and she'd been sent again, no doubt relaying some news which she hoped against hope would spur Rogon to action.

She rode to within inches of Rogon and swiftly dismounted.

The girl was young, no older than seventeen, and tufts of bright blonde hair escaped her scarf. If she ever ventured into southron territory she'd face terrible danger; every man, from every caste high and low, would want her.

"A word in private," she said.

She was used to having her demands met—even by Rogon, the Dark Captain.

In Rogon's tent, she pulled her headscarf, baring her

flowing golden hair and bright blue eyes.

"A word." There was worry in her voice, something that hadn't been there before.

"What do you have to say?"

His attempt at a charming smile didn't win her over. "Theron is close," she said, "and he is a danger to you, and everyone."

"Why don't you find him, then? Why is it my concern?" No matter how many times he said it, these Maids of Prophecy didn't listen.

He knew her answer, too. You can lure him, she'd say; he wants to fight you. But there were other concerns. And what offer would she try to use this time? Would she entice him with silver or gold bars? Would she offer to spend the night in his tent? Nothing was worth the distraction. He was on the cusp of total victory.

"I have it on good authority he plans to harm you… to thwart you…"

Rogon laughed. "Enough, woman. Leave the camp and never come back again."

In the span of a second a blade was up to Rogon's neck; the Maid of Prophecy was holding a cold steel dagger, pushing it so tight against his skin it threatened to cut him. "You have no idea who you're dealing with."

Without hesitation Rogon pushed her to the ground. Prostrate, she backed away, eyes full of terror.

Yet in Fharas, and even in this pederast nation, striking a woman was the height of dishonor; to kill a woman was worthy of ostracism. Rogon, the Dark Captain, had butchered entire towns; but even he had standards.

Trembling, the Maid of Prophecy was uttering platitudes, begging for mercy.

"Go," he said, "and never return."

She grabbed the scarf next to her and scrambled out of the tent. As she left, fear molting into anger, she cursed, "You have not heard the last of us…"

Rogon laughed darkly. If her words were true, there would be no mercy when she returned.

THE SUN KING'S ROAD, KERSICA

In the shade of palms, the heat was still unbearable, beating down through the carriage window—and though Gaia thought often of getting up and walking alongside her servants, she was not equipped for the task. Her slippers of gold cloth were inset with jewels that could easily be worn off; her slippers of wool would tear along the road. She could not keep pace with the horses. She would have to settle for her idleness.

She had brought books, entire stacks of them, but still had grown restless.

She had bought every book she could find on the archaic world, on the legends of the Old Dominion, on hagiography of the gods' so-called servants, but nothing had given her insight into the demiurge or his origins. Nothing had given her insight into this creature who had invaded her dreams and taken hold of her life.

Outside were Kersica's burning-hot plains. Off in the distance, near an outcropping of rocks, a Kersican in a crimson cape watched over his Elehoi. Shirtless and burnt by the sun, they swung pickaxes and broke up stone for their master, searching in vain for silver or gold.

Scenes like this reminded Gaia that there truly were fates worse than death. Living as a subhuman Elehoi was one of them.

When Korthos joined the Kersican League, there was much debate and dismay among some of Gaia's friends. Kersepolans' illiberal policies, their militarism, their inhumane treatment of the Elehoi, had inspired the hatred of the Korthian elite.

"Why," Gaia's friend Hippolyta asked, "are we friends with them now?"

Korthos didn't have much choice. Weakened by the Southron War, with a depleted army, accepting the Kersican League's protection was an afterthought.

The lockbox jerked to life. Soon the metal Gauntlet was pounding against the iron prison which entrapped it. Tears formed in Gaia's eyes, tears at this burden which she did not deserve to bear. She could handle heartbreak and poverty and disappointment, all the common human troubles; but to be haunted, to be possessed night after night, day after day, to be tormented by a creature from another realm—that was too much.

As she watched, tearfully, the lockbox jerk and shake, an idea came to her. What if she left the lockbox altogether? What if she buried it underground in the middle of the night?

She wept in silence.

~

Across the burning plains, beside dried-up riverbeds, and across the span of many nights and days, the carriage rolled on. It had disembarked in Korthos, a city which seemed impossibly far away.

At last, the road passed by Kersepoli. Its towering walls dwarfed the palms around it. The smell of sea salt was in the air.

It was the thirteenth of Alphaios.

Throughout country inns and by watering-holes where travelers gathered, the word had already spread; that the Dark Captain had encamped around Thénai after emerging unscathed from the mountain snows. Gaia was not surprised by his success; he succeeded in all he did. If she didn't expect success, she would not have begun this journey all these days and weeks ago.

And there were many miles to go.

A dirty river marked the border between Kersica and

Thenoa. Once, in happier times, the bridge had been unguarded. Now a fortress blocked entry to the other side, and battalions of Thenoan hoplites lined the river bank. The road, made of packed dirt, became gleaming white stone as soon as Thenoa began: its bright, meandering path shone in the sun against the golden hills.

The fortress was flying a blue-and-gold laurel wreath flag, indicating its allegiance to the Thenoan League.

Normally, in times of war, a carriage could pass through. But in this dark era, perhaps Gaia had misjudged.

She donned her slippers and took a look in the mirror, straightening a few curls from her hair.

She had one shot.

The leader of the battalions met her on the bridge.

"The way is shut," he said, but judging by the tone of his voice, it wasn't a sure thing.

"I have family in Thenoa," she said. She could not think of a name of one of Thénai's tiny villages. Perhaps she had best leave it at that."

"Thousands are dead," he said. The blue sash he wore over his breastplate was studded with medals of all kinds. He fancied himself a Stratego.

His face was grim.

"The fields are burning. Your family may be dead. Are you sure?" the man asked.

For a moment, Gaia regretted lying to this earnest man. And not for the first time, she was disgusted with Rogon's taste for violence and butchery. His soul was cold and uncaring. She knew it, she knew every part of him. "I have to go home," Gaia lied again. "I have to see."

The would-be Stratego left.

Not long afterwards, hoplite's emerged from the doors of the fort.

After rifling through the carriage for weaponry, they let the carriage go. She was only days from what she dreaded most: visiting Rogon, once her lover, whom she now hated more than anyone in the world.

FOOTHILLS OF MOUNT BARKALOS

The idea had seemed crazy from the start, but Theron wasn't in the habit of telling Khloë "no."

They entered a cavern and found, hidden in the darkness, a trapdoor. This, Khloë promised, led directly into the House of the Archon.

When Theron protested, telling her he had indeed lived in the House of the Archon, and never seen this, she still insisted.

"I don't think I'll be able to fit," Aigon said.

And it was true. There was no physical way for Aigon to drop into the trapdoor's opening, let alone crawl through the narrow, claustrophobic tunnel.

"We will hold our own," Theron said, though he would certainly feel more vulnerable without the hulking giant's protection. It was all well and good; he had a skull to crack, Kunar's.

~

The tunnels were dark and airless. Theron could scarcely breathe. His body brushed up against the sides of the walls, and though it was good to be with Khloë, more and more he regretted his decision to accompany her.

Thénai had betrayed him. He had saved them in the Thenoan War, and the populace—ungrateful and spoiled—had abandoned him for loving Daphnë.

Now his greatest friend was an amazon. Did he have a problem? Did something draw him to amazons—or did he draw them in?

The trek continued until Theron's sandals were worn and his legs ached, until he was out of breath and fatigued beyond words. At last the pitch-black, musty passageway gave way to an open chamber.

A private palace had been built here, overlooking a pool, but no one was in sight.

"Has he left?" Theron asked. He had come here to administer justice; but it looked like the gods had other plans.

"No," Khloë said, "follow me."

With a graceful ease she sidestepped around the pool and ran across the vast chamber, up a stone ramp and into yet another tunnel.

Theron sighed. He wasn't sure if he could bear another journey like the last one.

At some point in the darkness, Khloë stopped. Theron could hear the clattering of pots and pans, the shouting of servants, the footsteps of creaking wooden floorboards. They were within inches of the supposed painting which obscured the entryway.

But Theron put a hand on Khloë's and stopped her. He could not help but notice that the passageway went on. More places in the House of the Archon were connected to the secret tunnels.

Theron gestured ahead. Khloë, in the dim light that seeped through the tunnel, gave him a quizzical look. Then, just as soon, she obeyed.

The noise was omnipresent, varying in intensity as they passed through the dark passageways. Many times, Theron worried that someone would hear them and uncover the secret. But they pushed on, through a seemingly-endless number of twists and turns, until they reached the terminus.

Through an open door they walked... and into a closet.

Fur coats hung from a rack, alongside tunics and trousers of all shapes and sizes. Shoes and boots were piled on top of each other, forming a booby trapped floor. And from the room ahead, there were voices.

He recognized the voice of Kunar. He had heard his demagoguery once on the streets of Thénai. "Tonight," he said.

"We will get ready," said the voice of another. "I will let Rogon know. You have them posted at the gate?"

"At a moment's command," answered Kunar.

"Good… Athra be praised."

"Athra be praised," Kunar said.

Athra, the southron god, had been invoked. Had Eloesus truly fallen this far?

Whatever they spoke of had a whiff of conspiracy. Kunar had joined hands with Rogon. Had they struck a devil's bargain? Had he settled with Rogon, offering Thénai—the city which he had hoodwinked—for something else in return?

And the Thenoans, once Theron's fellow citizens, had voted for Kunar in all their numbers. Did they know, now, what a terrible mistake they'd made? Somehow Theron doubted it. They were happy in their ignorance, happy in their lack of knowledge. Surely the citizens ignored the signs that Kunar didn't have their best interests at heart.

It was not in Theron's nature to stand still and refuse to strike first. But though he held his club *Titan's Fist* in his hand, he remained quiet and rigid. What if he was wrong? What if he sent Thénai into chaos? What if the city fell, and it was because of him?

Before he could react, Khloë rushed ahead and Theron scrambled after.

"Amara!" Theron cursed.

As he burst out from the closet, he could see what had drawn Khloë from her hiding place. Her two sabers gleamed from a display case near the door.

Kunar ran out of the room, screaming.

"Was it worth it?" Theron said.

She smashed the glass of the display case and grabbed both sabers.

"Was it worth it?" Theron repeated at a shout.

As an alarm bell began to ring throughout the palace, and screaming echoed throughout the halls, Khloë ran her eyes over the sabers, smiled, and laughed. "Yes!" she said. "Yes, it was."

THE SUN KING'S ROAD, THENOA

The carriage had rattled along the road for three days since the river crossing. Gaia spent most nights unable to sleep, weeping at the shaking of the lockbox and of the Gauntlet which it hid.

At intervals, when she looked out the window into the hill country, she thought of burying it underground. But doing so would invite the wrath of the demiurge; he would haunt her dreams forever. One last act of obeisance, one last quest completed, and he would leave her alone forever—or so Gaia hoped. Could she really count on his promises? Could she really believe a word he uttered?

As a little girl, Gaia was told stories of how the hero Phillipidēs slew Kronos and tossed him into the fiery mountain. Now she knew, that was just a fable.

This burden she was bearing—she hoped to Amara and to the Goddess's attendants that it would be removed from her soon.

~

In the midst of the hill country, the road came to a crossing. The aptly-named Golden Road ran up and down the golden hills toward Thénai: a piercing beam of white stone amid the grass. Once heavily-trafficked, it was now almost empty, in view of burnt-out shells of farmhouses and corpses which rotted away in the hot sun. The trail of bloodshed Rogon left had destabilized and depopulated Thenoa. That, no doubt, was his intention.

As they embarked on the Golden Road, one hot afternoon on the cusp of summer, Gaia relished the thought of her pain coming to an end; but in her heart, she somehow doubted the demiurge would let her go. She would be cursed forever; this weight lying upon her would never be lifted.

HIGH CITY, THÉNAI

Theron burst out of the palace, breaking open the door; and blood followed him, dripping out onto the stone steps. *Titan's Fist* had created a slaughter in the once-hallowed halls, and together with Khloë he had eliminated all threats. She stepped out ahead of him, onto the High City, her sabers dripping red.

An alarm bell was ringing; but Kunar was gone.

Hoplites could be seen in the distance, their blue capes rustling in the wind; but they didn't charge Theron or even draw their spears and shields.

He could not see their faces behind their helms; but perhaps they recognized Theron. Clearly, they had such little respect for their coward king that they didn't rush to attack.

Now leaderless, the city would surely fall, unless someone rallied the troops.

Theron rushed ahead, running to the edge of the High City; and saw Kunar's fat form descending at a mad pace toward Thénai's streets.

The hoplites watched him in silence. Between the army and Theron, it seemed they were on the same side. Kunar had abandoned Thénai; and Theron would protect it.

LION'S GATE, THÉNAI

Dusk was settling in over the hills, painting the leonine figures and griffins on Thénai's most famous gate in shadow. Even in the dimming light, the gate was a masterwork of stone and wood; the two lions, facing each other, on the gate's lintel were so detailed each hair on their bodies was defined.

When the last light of sun filtered through, Kunar would open the gate. The king would betray the people, and deliver the city into Rogon's hands.

Yet as the last of the light filtered away, and the sun sank below the city wall, the gate did not budge.

The battalions Rogon had summoned to the Lion's Gate were looking at him disrespectfully. *He's gone mad,* they were surely thinking. *Kunar's played a trick on him.*

But Rogon was a good judge of character and intention. Kunar had meant every word.

~

When the stars were shining and the crescent moon glowed overhead, a towering figure appeared on the city wall. In one hand he held a torch, illuminating a lion's skin which he wore on his head. In the other he held a corpse by the neck.

Rogon backed away and took in a cold gasp.

This was Theron.

This was Theron, and that sighting of him he'd witnessed was not a dream.

That night, when he'd conjured up a great fire for the Nameless God, he had been within inches of Theron. He could have slain him then.

It had not been a vision. It had not been a dream. It was real.

"Here is Chairos!" Theron shouted from the heights. "The gatekeeper, who would have betrayed his city! You and Kunar bought him for a price! Now claim him!" He tossed the corpse from the battlements; it fell all those fathoms and broke to pieces in blood and bone.

Rogon's stunned silence, in an instant, was replaced by anger. "Kill him!" he screamed, and arrows flew, but Theron took shelter behind the parapets.

Then Theron stood up. A rock was in his hand. He had dropped the torch.

With a cry he hurled the stone at Rogon and struck him head-on.

Unconscious, Rogon sank to the floor. His men scattered, and panic overtook the ranks.

LION'S GATE, THÉNAI

One afternoon, when the sun was blazing and Gaia—half asleep in the carriage—had lost track of the days and weeks she'd been in transit, they reached Thénai.

At the news Gaia leapt to her feet, threw on her slippers and rushed outside.

There was no siege; there was no army encamped around the city walls.

The Lion's Gate was open wide to traffic.

And in the shadow of the wall, there was a black form, wheezing and barely clinging to life.

In a rush, Gaia leapt back into the carriage and grabbed the lockbox. She took a deep breath and exited quietly. "Go on without me," she ordered her servants. "Find the nearest inn. I'll meet you there."

She waited until the carriage was out of sight; and then she walked over to the Dark Captain, once her lover, who—in his frailty—she realized she still had feelings for.

Like a giant bug he appeared, in his antennaed helmet and bulky black-plated armor. He was white and clearly malnourished. He was close to death.

She set the lockbox next to him.

"Oh, Rogon," she whispered. She stooped over him. The life had seeped out of his pallid face. He was close to death.

His army had abandoned him. He had spoken often of their undying loyalty, how he could rely on them, even to march to their deaths…

How wrong he was. As soon as he fell, his soldiers scattered in every direction, leaving him to suffer and die.

How ironic that Gaia, the one who hated him most, was the only one left to tend to him.

Rogon's eyes opened. The man was paralyzed. He tried to speak but all that came out was a low, strained groan. He was wheezing.

She stooped over to kiss him, but stopped an inch from his lips. How could she forget his betrayal? How could she forget his scorn? How could she forget the embarrassment and shame he'd put her through?

She remembered again the truth: how she hated him more than anyone in this world.

The words of the *demiurge* echoed in her mind: "to him whom thou hatest most, give it."

With a key she opened the lockbox and pulled the Gauntlet of the Demiurge out.

The shimmering black metal weighed heavy on her arms. With both hands she set it before Rogon and – ignoring his pained protests – removed his iron glove.

On the left hand, where she'd guess it would pain him the most, she slid the Gauntlet of the Demiurge.

Runes and glyphs, once invisible to the naked eye, burst into light. Metal melded to skin; the Gauntlet tightened and bonded to Rogon's arm. Rogon screamed, even as control of his body returned—he screamed and flailed, now able to move again. The Gauntlet had replaced his weakness with a new, dark strength.

Gaia stepped back in panic. Her heart exploded in her chest as the Dark Captain once again stood on his feet.

The Gauntlet had grown in size now that it had a new victim. "Go, Gaia." Rogon's voice was deeper than before and loud as a shout. "Run…"

Without a second's thought, Gaia heeded the warning, bolting toward the safety of Thénai. Lion's Gate welcomed her as she ran into the teeming crowds, but nothing could take away the terror of what she'd just seen, the horror of what she'd just witnessed.

HIGH CITY, THÉNAI

They had offered him the kingship.

They had offered him the city.

They had offered him the world.

Theron turned down each offer.

He had saved Thénai, but this was not his fight.

He did not want to lead Thénai; he did not want to save it. This was not his world.

Looking out from the High City, Mount Barkalos was visible. Aigon was nowhere to be found. It seemed he had abandoned Theron.

The Thenoans had offered Khloë the kingship, and the city and everything she desired; but she too had turned down each offer. "My place is with you," Khloë had said.

Where to go next? What was Theron's next adventure? He had chosen a hero's life, the life of a nomad.

In the distance, blended into a crowd, was a woman in a blue hooded gown. She had a dagger in her hand.

It was time to go.

THÉNAI HARBOR

Debris was floating in the water and the scattered remnants of burned-up ships tossed to-and-fro. Yet merchant vessels were passing to and from the port; and from her position on the foredeck, Bat Zor could see a city bursting with life.

It would not be so forever. She had seen the city's destruction in her dreams.

Hidden in a veil and a cloak, not even these sailors knew she accompanied them.

Yet Hyron, the now-dead Archon of Thénai, had called for her here.

Help, Thénai asked of Tharta. Help, they would not get. They would get Bat Zor.

EPILOGUE

Aigon watched from a distance as Rogon's army splintered and broke up, running away in every direction.

Theron had won the day.

But Aigon could accompany his young ward no longer. Aigon had drawn too much attention already. The best way to protect Theron was to leave him alone.

Hours later a shadowy form came running from Thénai's walls. He recognized the fat form instantly: Kunar, the would-be king.

The centaurs, in ancient days, were hunters. Aigon had not lost his passion for it.

He nocked an arrow to his bow and took off in pursuit. It was time to hunt. His prey was slipping away.

CONTINUED IN BOOK 7, 'WAR OF KINGS'

GLOSSARY

CALENDAR

1: Alphaios (March)

2: Pheidos (April)

3: Dektros (May)

4: Soloön (June)

5: Tyron (July)

6: Amaron (August)

7: Ergon (September)

8: Nichion (October)

9: Phimetron (November)

10: Kryon (December)

11: Titanion (January)

12: Etapion (February)

CURRENCY

Thalos: A small silver coin, worth one-fourth a *doukos*. Plural *thalon*.
Doukos: The standard silver coin across Eloesus. It takes many forms but generally has the city's patron god cast onto the front and the victory laurel wreath on the back. Plural *doukon*. One *doukos* is about the daily wage of a skilled laborer.
Oros: A gold coin, worth fifty *doukon*. Plural *orhon*.
Talent: A unit of measurement, worth one-thousand *doukon*.

TERMS

Academy, the: Originally an informal gathering at an olive grove in Korthos, it has assumed the makings of an organization. Money has begun to enrich the founders of the Academy, allowing them to construct a building and pay their teachers.

Alabastros: The king of the gods in the Eloesian pantheon. He is revered especially by the Thartans. As king of the gods, he is considered to preside over kingship, leadership, and royalty. He is often depicted as a wise old man. His favored animal is the lion

Amara: The goddess of motherly love in the Eloesian pantheon. In Thénai and the Amazonian Isles, she is also the goddess of wisdom and battle. Although a mother, she is a virgin. Eloesian legend states she is the daughter of Alabastros and the Earth. Her brother is Tyros, god of war.

Amazons, the: A race of people living in the coastal islands off the Eloesian shore. Their women are far stronger and—some argue—more intelligent than their men. Though they look similar to humans, amazons and humans cannot breed. The child of an amazon and a human is always stillborn.

Amazonia: A term for amazon lands. Amazonia encompasses the islands of Jogheira, Straiteira, Agathë, Kalormenë and a few smaller islands.

Archaic World, the: A term generally referring to the time period before the Amazon-Eloesian War, circa 50 years before the consecration of the temple (B.C.T.) or before the Fall of Stygia, ten years later.

Arkadion: A village, the largest in the wilds of Themuria, called the Bride of the Wilderness. It is allied to Kersepoli.

Barbarian: A non-Eloesian. The Isteroi and the people of the Ten Cities are often considered barbarians.

Chiton: A knee-length sleeveless shirt, once popular across Eloesus but now restricted to priests and government officials.

Civic gods: The gods considered sacred to a particular city. Tharta favors Alabastros; Korthos, Nix and Arephon; Kersepoli, Tyros lord of war; and Thénai, Amara.

Courtesans: In Eloesus, the uppermost tier of all prostitutes—though all are considered low class. They are chosen by elite courtesans' guilds and taught—in addition to the art of lovemaking—the harp or lyre, as well as conversation. Because of this, they are often the most educated of Eloesian women, who are usually encouraged to stay at home.

Demiarch: In the cities of Korthos and Thénai, members of the Assembly.

Elehoi: A large underclass, forming the majority of the population of Kersica. They are slaves, captives from Kersepoli's numerous wars, and all Eloesian by birth. The name means "little Eloesian" or "Eloesian-like."

Fharas: A vast empire, by far the strongest power in the world. It is ruled by the King of Kings, who is considered a living god. The word Fharas and Fharese also refers to a certain region and people—the heartland where the empire began.

Fharaizing: A program of close trade links and cultural shift started by King Gygax I, the father of the current king of Tharta. In Fharaization, Tharta would join a close alliance with the southrors and welcome their temples and cultural influence.

Fields of Paradise: According to Eloesian religion, a region of heaven where the heroes and certain virtuous mortals go after death.

Free and Democratic Army of Thénai, the: The name of Thénai's army, composed mostly of everyday citizens. As part of schooling, every man is taught to lift a shield and march in formation. The army is led by a Stratego, or general.

High city: A common feature of all Eloesian cities, a towering high ground—natural or man made—which serves as a fortress in times of trouble.

Hoplite: The traditional soldier in the Eloesian army. Each hoplite has a helmet and a breastplate, a spear and a shortsword, in addition to an iron-rimmed wooden shield. When fighting, he locks shields with his fellow hoplites, forming an impenetrable wall as long as he holds formation.

Ink-of-Tyrhenos: A cosmetic product created from squid's ink, used to darken eyelashes and hair. It is named after Tyrhenos, the legendary king of the cyclops, for reasons unknown.

Isdar: The goddess of fertility and carnal desire. She once had a large temple in Tharta, where sacred prostitutes were employed. This was shut down in the reign of the Fharaizing king, Gygax I.

Isteroi: See Isteros.

Isteros: A region in the north of Eloesus, along the river Ister. The Isteroi speak a dialect of Eloesian but are thought to be outsiders, due to their pallid complexions and frequently red hair. Arctos, the capital, is much smaller in size than other Eloesian cities.

Kersepoli: A large city, one of the four greatest in Eloesus. It is the most militaristic of the Eloesian cities and is ruled by two kings, either of whom may overrule the other.

Kersica: The region belonging to the city of Kersepoli.

Korthica: The lands belonging to Korthos.

Korthos: A large city, one of the four greatest in Eloesus. It is ruled by an Assembly, elected by the people, and an archon, elected by the Assembly.

Lion's Gate, the: The main gate of Thénai. Two lions are carved in stone above its giant double doors.

Magi: The priesthood of Fharas. They worship the god of fire, Athra, and revere all flames as sacred. Only youth with magical talent are chosen; they are taught both about the god Athra and also the skill of conjuring and controlling fire. Since magical talent is rare and can be found among the peasantry, becoming a magus is one of the few opportunities for advancement in Fharas's class-based society.

Mount Agni: A mountain in Fharas. The magi have their temple on the slopes.

Nix: The goddess of secrets and whispers, her followers call her the Gray Lady or the Queen of Sorcery. She presides over the knowledge of herbs—healing and poisonous—as well as hidden knowledge, wisdom, and the metals iron and silver. She is feared throughout Eloesus, though her name is invoked for protection from the unquiet dead. Korthos was historically the center of her worship. Her favored animals are the owl and the dog. According to Eloesian legend, she is the daughter of Tyros, god of war, and Seladora, goddess of nature. She was hated by her parents and cast out of the household.

Nissos: A remote island off the coast of Eloesus, the center of the slave trade.

Old Dominion, the: A legendary empire which was said to rule the entire world. It was destroyed suddenly, in one night, by fire and ash. Its cities sank into the sea.

Phillipidēs: An Eloesian legendary hero, the son of a Thartan noble who fought in the Megarine War. According to myth, he was given a magic helmet by the goddess Amara which made him invincible to mortal weapons.

Politarch: In the cities of Eloesus, these are the government officials answerable directly to the Assembly. They are charged with certain categories of oversight; thus one politarch might manage the food supply, the other the water. In Korthos and Thénai, they are appointed by the Assembly; in Kersepoli and Tharta they are appointed by kings. Their duties vary from one city to the other.

Slavery: The institution is widespread in Fharas and offers slaves no rights whatsoever; they are viewed as objects or tools, not human beings. In Eloesus, the institution is banned altogether in Thénai and heavily regulated in Korthica and Thartica. Slaves have no rights in Kersepoli. In Kersepoli, most slaves are war captives and called Elehoi.

Southrons: A term for the Fharese, Khazideans, and more generally people from the far south.

Sirens: Aquatic creatures which dwell in the seas off Eloesus. They resemble a cross between woman and fish, with green-scaled skin and a fish's tail. They can sing beautifully and entice sailors through mind-affecting scents which they give off, luring victims into a deadly embrace. Sirens—being carnivores—love nothing more than dragging a sailor into the depths to devour him.

Stygia: An ancient region which was named after the now-vanished city-state of Stygidos.

Stratego: In the Eloesian military, a general or commander.

Tharta: A great city, considered the chief in Eloesus. It is ruled by a king but has certain limited forms of democracy.

Thartica: The lands belonging to Tharta. The region allows for extensive irrigation which results in plentiful food.

Themuria: A region of Eloesus, wild and undeveloped. Being at a much higher altitude than the coast, snow is common in the winter. The region's chief town is Arkadion.

Thénai: A large city, one of the four greatest in Eloesus. It is ruled by an Assembly, elected by the people, and an archon, elected by the Assembly.

Thenoa: The lands belonging to Thénai.

Ten Cities: A confederation of ten city-states, west from Eloesus across a desert, with Megaris as its head. The Ten Cities take great pride in their half-southron, half-Eloesian identity. They say they form a bridge between Fharese despotism and Eloesian democracy.

Tigris: The largest city of the Amazons, having about thirty thousand residents plus half as many slaves. It is located on the island of Jogheira. The amazon queen, Daphnë, rules from here.

Tyros: The god of war. He is revered in Kersepoli and Isteros; yet he is viewed as never favoring one city over the other, delighting only in battle itself and spilled blood. According to Eloesian legend, he was the son of Alabastros and the Earth. His sister is Amara and his daughter is Nix, whom he hates.

ABOUT THE AUTHOR

Cursed at birth with a wild imagination, Andrew Cooper spent his youth dreaming of worlds more exciting than Earth.

He is a graduate of the Odyssey Writing Workshop. His stories have appeared in Morpheus Tales, Fear and Trembling, Residential Aliens and Mindflights, among others.

CONTACT THE AUTHOR

Visit **www.aj-cooper.com** to sign up for the newsletter and stay up-to-date on new releases.

Find him on Facebook at:

www.facebook.com/AJCooperauthor

www.ingramcontent.com/pod-product-compliance
Lightning Source LLC
Chambersburg PA
CBHW031247210726
48287CB00003B/930